Killian

MEGAN FALL

A Fallen Angel Novel
Book 1

D1713781

Table of Contents

Blurb

Killian is an Angel of Death. His assignment is to amass souls and take them to heaven. He isn't allowed to let the humans see him, and he isn't allowed to determine their fate.

When he heads out to collect a soul and encounters a beautiful girl being beaten, he can't help but step in and save her. But, because of his interference he's cast out of heaven, stripped of his wings, and sent spiralling to earth.

A month later he finds the girl, but she's now being hunted. Her time was up, and other paranormals have descended to complete his task that he left unfinished. Not only that, but a prophesy has come to light, and it appears Killian is destined to mate and produce a heir that will unite all paranormals.

Will a Fallen Angel be powerful enough to save the girl he's come to love? And is she his prophesied mate? Things aren't always what they same, and the couple must decide if love is worth risking it all.

Chapter 1
Killian

Killian glided on the tails of the wind. His massive wings held straight out from his sides. The black feathers shimmered in the setting sun, as its rays bounced off them. He was dressed only in black leather pants, and his chest was on display. His powerful muscles were decorated with swirling patterns of black ink. His black hair hung below his shoulders in messy waves, and blew wildly around his face in the wind.

He circled the area as he flew overhead. He scanned the alleys below, peering into their dark depths. He was an angel of death and his target was somewhere below. He was given her name by the council, and once he had it an image of her instantly formed in his head. She would die tonight, and he would be there to safely take her soul to heaven.

Killian turned quickly, tilting his massive wings and dipping down. He could sense her and knew she was close. The area repulsed him. Bars littered the streets and the smell was horrid. Music pumped from their darkened depths and intoxicated patrons stumbled from their doors.

He caught movement in one of the alleys and immediately knew he'd found her. He flew straight for it, flapping his giant wings and stirring up the garbage below. The humans looked up, as they stumbled from the gust of wind he produced when he flew past them. He wasn't worried, they couldn't see him. The girl would be the only one that would be able to, and that was only after she had taken her final breath.

He finally spotted her at the end of one of the alleys. It appeared as though a man had dragged her back there, and the dumpster they were behind hid them from view. He could clearly see the man was up to no good. The girl was thrashing and sobbing as the man rained blow after blow on her tiny body. Her long brown hair lay in a tangled mess around her, and Killian could see her clothing had been torn.

Death angels didn't have any feelings, but something penetrated his frigid heart as he watched the scene below. He almost felt sorry for the pretty girl. Her death wouldn't be an easy one, and it would be painfully drawn out. No one could hear her screams. She wouldn't be getting any help.

Killian dropped to the ground beside them, breaking the concrete underneath his bare feet. He hated landing. The ground could never hold his weight. His arms lowered and his wings closed as they tucked in close to his back. He prowled closer to the scene in front of him. The girl wasn't struggling as much now, and her screams were quieting. It wouldn't be long now before she was released from this world.

Suddenly, his whole body tensed as she looked directly into his eyes and begged him for help. He was stunned and could only stare back at her. She shouldn't be able to see him. No human had seen an angel of death before they passed. But sure enough she could. She proved it by reaching out with her tiny bloodied hand in his direction.

The assailant moved off her and went for his belt. It was clear to Killian the man intended to rape her before delivering the death blow. The girl softly whimpered and tried to drag her broken body towards him. She moved painstakingly slow, and blood coated the ground below her.

Killian watched her, his mind reeling. He'd never cared before about any of his targets, but for some reason the thought of the man violating her that way infuriated him. He took a step towards the girl then stopped. He had explicit instructions never to interfere. She looked up at him pleadingly as her hand fell to the ground limply. Then watched as tears tumbled from her eyes.

The man had his pants undone now, and was bending to push them out of the way. He sneered at the girl as she cowered before him. The man took one step towards her, and as if on autopilot Killian took one step towards them. The girls eyes snapped back to him as they caught the movement.

"Please," she whispered as the man bent over her once more.

Killian knew the dress she wore had been beautiful at one time, but now it was destroyed. The man grabbed it in his greasy fists and tore it down the middle. Her lacy white bra glowed in the darkness and drew his attention. She looked so innocent wearing that colour. The man was pawing and scratching at her breasts in his excitement.

Killian's heart stammered and his firsts clenched. He glanced at the tiny girl once more. Her eyes were squeezed shut tightly, and her face was scrunched up in pain. Confused, he looked back at the man. The man was pushing her dress up and tearing at her white panties.

Killian had seen enough. He roared so loud the ground shook, as he flew at the man. He reached out with his massive fists and hit the man's chest as he kept his forward momentum. The man smashed into the brick wall behind him and dented it, as his body was crushed from the impact. Bricks flew in all directions and blood poured from the man's mouth as he looked up at Killian in horror. Then his eyes closed and he crumpled to the ground. Killian knew immediately he was dead, and for the first time in his life he smiled.

Chapter 2
Tabby

Tabby looked up at the massive man that was standing in the alley not too far away. She could feel the power emanating from his muscled body, and it frightened her. She was confused, as she hadn't seen him arrive. She'd heard a loud boom and felt the ground shake, and then he was just there.

Another blow was delivered to her side, and she cried out in pain. She begged the man to help her, but he only stared at her intently. He didn't move even an inch as he tilted his head and studied them. She noticed he only wore black leather pants, no shoes and no shirt, but she didn't have time to dwell on it as her attacker struck out again.

Tabby didn't come to this section of town very often, but tonight she had no choice. The bartender from the hole her father frequented called, ordering her to pick up his drunken ass and take him home. She had parked as close as she could, and was steps from the bar when she was grabbed from behind and dragged into the alley.

She screamed, but it fell on deaf ears. There was no one around to help. And, the ones that did hear her cry, simply didn't care. Her attacker didn't ask for money, which frightened her more. He simply threw her to the filthy ground and began to beat her. She fought hard at first, but the man was strong, and the numerous blows were taking their toll on her tiny body.

Tabby glanced at the stranger again. He was still staring at her, but he looked confused. His massive chest was covered in swirling ink and it vibrated with intensity. She was loosing her voice from screaming so long, but she tried to beg for his help again. He looked like he was struggling with some internal battle as he continued to stare at her.

She turned back to her attacker as his weight disappeared. When he stood she assumed he was done with her, but she wasn't that lucky. His hands immediately went to his belt and she looked up at him in horror. When the belt was undone and he was pulling down the zipper, she started to sob. She knew she was going to die in this alley, and she was terrified of all that would happen to her first.

Turning to the stranger, Tabby reached out her hand to him as she tried to drag her broken body closer. The pain was excruciating, and she knew she had suffered numerous broken bones from her attackers fists. Her body suddenly gave out, and she lay there in defeat, as her attacker once again covered her frame with his own.

Tabby barely registered what was happening as he tore at her dress. The cold night air hit her skin and instantly chilled her. His fingernails scraped her breasts and his breath singed her cheek. She sobbed as she felt her dress being pushed up and her panties tear.

Then she was free, as his body was ripped from hers. The stranger was throwing him against the wall. She felt the thud when he hit and heard bones breaking as her attacker smashed into it, then fell limply to the ground. Tears fell from her eyes as she stared at his now dead body.

The stranger turned then and looked down at her. She saw the fury on his face and wondered if he had killed the man so he could have her for himself. She couldn't move, so she could only watch as he approached. He knelt down and reached towards her. Tabby whimpered as she shook her head no, unsure of his intentions.

He ignored her reaction, and she trembled as his warm fingers touched her sides. Slowly he pulled at her dress, until the torn pieces were crossed against her and she was modestly covered. Then he reached down and pulled at the bottom, until it fell to her knees. Tabby gazed at him in awe as he wiped the tears from her face, then simply stared at his wet hand in fascination.

In a move so quick she almost didn't he see it, she was scooped up and pulled into his warm chest. He climbed to his feet with her in his arms, then took three quick steps and leaped. She cried out in fright as massive black wings appeared from the back of his body and flapped, lifting them high into the night sky.

Tabby shivered, and she had no idea if it was from fear or the cold wind, but he must have felt it because he curled his powerful body around hers. She looked down at the city below, and was mesmerized by the sight, when she suddenly noticed it seemed to be getting closer quickly. She buried her face in his neck and held on as they descended.

There was a loud thump as they landed, and she swore she heard the concrete crack, but surprisingly she wasn't jarred at all. Tabby looked up at him at the same time he looked down at her, and they both studied each other. She couldn't believe that an angel had saved her. Maybe he was a guardian angel. But then why had he waited so long before stepping in.

Gently, he lowered her to the ground, and the cold concrete seeped into her small body. She shivered, and wished he'd pick her up again. Then he bent over her and with surprising tenderness brushed her tangled hair out of her face. She closed her eyes when his warm lips brushed her forehead.

When she opened them again he was gone, and only the cracked cement remained as proof that he was even there. She looked around and realized he had dropped her at the door of a hospital. Then she gave into the darkness as staff members rushed out and headed her way.

Chapter 3
Killian

Killian soared on the gust of wind as he shot like a bullet straight up into the sky. His wings were tucked close to his body and his head was raised upward. He had been summoned by Azriel, and you did not keep the guardian of the angels of death waiting. As he hit the end of the gust he let out his powerful wings and flapped them so his momentum would continue. Up he rose, higher and higher into the clear blue sky. The city became a spec far below.

He broke through the clouds and came out the other side, to land at the white gates of heaven. He hated being up here, and he hated being around other angels. That's why he loved his job so much, he loved the solitude it provided him. The guard nodded as he approached and opened the gates enough for Killian to slip through. After he passed through them, the guard slammed them shut once more. He made his way to Azriel's main office and threw the doors open without bothering to knock.

"What was so important you pulled me away from my list?" Killian barked. "I had three more souls to collect before I came back here," he grunted in annoyance.

Azriel pushed away from his desk and stood, moving until they were toe to toe. The angels were the same height, and were able to look each other directly in the eyes.

"Tabitha Bray was on your list, but somehow late yesterday evening she was found on the steps of St. Vincent's Hospital. And, we have a soul that arrived when it wasn't his time. Care to explain what the hell you thought you were doing? You know we don't play god. We collect the souls on the list and we move onto the next one," Azriel spat. "You've always done well at your job. You've been one of my best angels."

Killian hung his head in submission. "I couldn't do it. Maybe I'm just tired of taking souls who shouldn't be taken. She was beautiful, and so innocent, she didn't deserve to be taken so young. The scumbag who was hurting her though, he deserved to die. One human," he angrily sneered. "I saved one human and I get called by you."

"You broke the cardinal rule. Never get involved. You had a job to do and you didn't complete it. For that, you need to be punished."

"Punished," Killian growled in complete surprise. "For caring for a human enough to not want to see her die? You always tell me I'm too cold and unfeeling. The one time I listen you feel the need to punish me for it."

Killian watched as Azriel lifted a silver, long handled blade from his desk. "For breaking our most important rule I sentence you to live the rest of your life as a fallen. You will be stripped of your wings and will be forced to walk the rest of your days with the humans. I'm sorry my old friend," Azriel apologized softly.

Before Killian could blink he was behind him. Azriel lifted the blade and a searing pain ran down the length of his back. He roared in both anguish and torment as his wings were sliced clean from this body. He dropped to his knees, wracked with agony, as his beautiful wings fell to the floor. Killian had heard it was like torture having your wings cut off, and now he believed. It felt like a part of him had been severed from his body.

Killian stared at them in horror as they lost their beautiful shimmer and turned a dull, lifeless grey colour. He had always taken pride in his wings, and the sight of them like that broke something in him.

Then Azriel was kneeling beside him. He placed his palm flat on his forehead and a blinding light flashed through the room. Killian screamed, as the floor suddenly dropped out from beneath him.

He blinked, and when he opened his eyes he found himself in a free fall, heading straight to the earth. He bellowed as his back felt like it had been torn open. His arms flailed and the wind took away his ability to breathe, and still he continued to fall.

He had no idea how long he fell for. To him it felt like hours. Until, finally he smashed into the ground, caving in the earth all around him. It felt like he had fallen into a huge crater. Dust rose all around him and he choked on it. He closed his eyes as the pain became unbearable and let the darkness take him.

But, just as he passed out, he pictured the beautiful human girl's face. He hoped like hell she was worth it, because he was going hunting when he woke up and he was going to find her. He fell because of her, and that meant she was his whether she wanted him or not. He was coming for her.

Chapter 4
Tabby

Tabby woke slowly, a steady beeping noise bringing her around. She had no idea where she was, but she knew without a doubt it wasn't her bedroom in the small apartment she rented. Carefully she opened her eyes, but the bright light caused them to burn and start running. She closed them again quickly and gave herself a few minutes. The next time she tried to open them she did it carefully, blinking several times until they adjusted to the light.

Finally, she was able to open them completely. She glanced around, groaning when she realized it was a hospital room. She had prayed everything she experienced had been just a dream. Apparently, it wasn't. She took stock of her body. She ached and was exhausted, but nothing hurt overly bad. Then she noticed the drip, and figured something in there was definitely helping to diminish the pain.

A nurse walked in then and Tabby watched her as she crossed the room. The first thing the nurse did was check the drip bag. Then she brought her a glass of water with a straw, which Tabby gratefully drank.

"How are you feeling my dear?" the nurse questioned as she pulled back the blankets to check her injuries.

"Sore and tired," Tabby told her. She watched as the nurse came closer to check her face.

"You came in here yesterday," she suddenly frowned. "And your face was a mess. Today those bruises look like they're about a week old." With a confused look on her face the nurse then peered at her arms. "All the scratches are gone, and the bruising on them is the same as your face."

The nurse turned quickly and suddenly pushed down on Tabby's stomach.

"Hey," Tabby painfully cried out. "That hurts."

The nurse stared at her and paled. "You should be screaming right now and passing out from the pain. You have five broken ribs," she explained with terrified eyes. "Yet you act as if they're only bruised." The nurse warily backed away from the bed and headed for the door. "I'm getting the doctor," she announced. "This can't be happening." Then the nurse turned and fled from the room.

Tabby understood that whatever just happened, she couldn't let the doctor examine her. She knew her injuries had been bad, and she knew she had been about to die. So, what had happened to her? She wondered if maybe her guardian angel had done something to her. But, one thing was for sure, she certainly wasn't sticking around here to find out.

Quickly, she pulled the IV from her arm. It stung and bled a bit, but she ignored it. Then she threw the covers off and jumped from the bed. Her ribs ached, but she ignored that too. She ran to the cabinet in the corner and pulled open the doors. Sitting on a shelf in a bag were her clothes. She hurried to the bathroom and ripped off the horrid hospital gown. It took her a minute to get her dress on as she was still pretty sore. She had to tie it in the front to hold the ripped pieces together, then she hurried back into the room and peeked out the door.

Everyone was going about their business and no one was watching her. She casually left the room and headed for the elevator. It seemed to take forever for it to come, and when it did, the dinging noise scared her half to death. In minutes she was hurrying through the front doors and headed down the sidewalk.

In her haste to get to the bar and collect her father she had left her purse at home, only grabbing her keys as she darted out the door. She reached in her pocket and sure enough the small key ring was still there. But, without her purse she had no money to use to get home.

It took her over an hour to walk from the hospital to her tiny apartment, and she was ready to drop when she got there. She hurried in the front doors and stopped at the elevator. When she pushed the button and it lit up, she almost did a first pump.

Some days the elevator didn't work at all, and today she figured would be one of those days. She lived on the sixth floor, and if she had to walk up them today, she was sure she would have cried.

When the elevator arrived she climbed on and waited the almost five minutes it took to reach her floor. When the doors started to open she got impatient, and slid out the crack before they opened completely.

Tabby's apartment was at the end of the hall, and as she got closer she knew something was wrong. She slowed down, and when she reached it she noticed the door was hanging at a funny angle. Carefully, she pushed it aside and stepped in.

When she looked around she couldn't help but cry at what she saw. Things were thrown everywhere, cushions were ripped, and water and dirt littered the floor from all her plants and flowers. The apartment had been destroyed, and even some of the drywall had been torn off the walls.

Now what was she supposed to do, she wondered. Who was after her? And what the hell had the angel done to her? With no answers she headed to her room, grabbed her backpack, and loaded it with what clothes she could salvage from the floor. Next, she pulled up the floorboard under her nightstand and yanked out her purse. Her apartment had been broken into before, so she'd learned to hide it well.

She hurried into the bathroom and changed out of her ripped dress. Then pulled on some jeans and a t-shirt. She threw some bathroom supplies in her bag quickly, put her long hair in a messy bun, and said goodbye to her life.

When Tabby headed out the door, she made sure not to look back.

Chapter 5
Tabby

The first thing Tabby decided do after leaving her apartment, was head to the bank. If someone was after her she needed cash to get away. Also, she didn't want to leave a trail that someone could follow, so cash it was. It was a fifteen minute walk to the bank, but she made it in ten.

She lined up and waited for an available teller, as she kept an eye on the door. She had no idea if someone might have been following her when she left the apartment. Finally, a teller was free, and Tabby was able to move up to the counter.

When she told the lady she wanted to withdraw all the money from her account, the lady gave her a hard time. She wanted to know why? She wanted to know if she was happy with the banks services? And, she wanted to know if she could put it into something else?

Frustrated, Tabby lied and told the teller her father was dying and she needed the money to pay his medical bills. Finally, the teller apologized and handed over an envelope of cash. There was almost four thousand dollars inside, and that was all the money she had to her name. She took it and hurried out of the bank.

Tabby decided the next thing she needed to do was to see if her car was where she left it. Again she decided to walk, not wanting to spend a dime of her money on either the bus or a taxi. It was a good twenty-five minute walk, but she figured she better get used to that. She had left her car in a city parking lot, and she approached it cautiously. When she was close she decided to stay back where she couldn't be seen, and watch it for while.

Tabby could tell the window had been broken, but at least it was still there. She sighed, whoever had trashed her apartment had probably trashed her car too. She was there almost a half hour before she noticed the man. He was leaning against a building across the street, and he was reading a paper.

She watched him for about ten minutes, and noticed that he didn't turn the page once. But, he glanced up at her car a dozen times. He didn't look around or get distracted by the many people passing by. He simply watched her car.

Tabby studied him. He was a tall man and looked to be in his mid thirties. He wore jeans and a t-shirt and his blond hair was long, falling well past his shoulders. He looked normal enough, but after seeing an angel she wasn't sure of anything anymore. She looked to her car again, and wondered if she could get to it and drive it out of the parking lot without him noticing. Probably not she figured.

When she looked back at the man he was staring right at her. She backed up two steps and hit the side of the building. He dropped his paper in the trash can beside him and pushed off the wall, heading across the street towards her.

Tabby gave a little yelp then turned and ran. Her ribs were screaming at her, but she ignored them and kept running. She ran down the street, staying away from the alleys this time. She could hear his feet on the cement behind her. He was gaining on her quickly.

Tabby turned into a residential area and headed for the park at the end of the street. She had just reached it when she was hit from behind. She crashed to the ground and rolled, popping up to see him crouched slightly over and staring at her curiously. He tilted his head to the side.

"I hear you survived a death angel," he growled at her as claws sprouted from his hands. She stared at his hands in terror and couldn't look away. She took a step back and he matched her step.

"No one has ever survived a death angel before," he growled. "I'm curious to know how you did it?" This time he was the first to move towards her, and she immediately took another step back.

Suddenly, he stretched out and took a slice at her with his claws. She screamed as a long deep cut was opened on her arm. She turned to run, when a huge gust of wind caught her and threw her back to the ground. She looked up to see an angel standing there, but this wasn't the one from the alley.

"You're on the list," he ominously declared. "Killian didn't take you, but I will."

Tabby started to crab crawl backwards, when a huge growl caught her attention. She turned in time to see clothing tear, and then a massive wolf stood where the man that had been chasing her only a minute ago was.

"She's mine," the beast growled almost unrecognizably.

Then he charged right at the angel. The two rolled to the ground, battling viciously. Tabby stood and scooped up her backpack then she ran again, as far away from the angel and wolf as she could get. She headed for her car, knowing she needed something faster than her feet.

She never looked back, knowing she would most likely hear them coming. She ran, and ran, finally reaching the car. The window was broken and the doors were unlocked, so she yanked it open and climbed inside. In minutes, she was tearing out of the parking lot and driving away. She had no idea where she was headed, but she knew she had to get as far away as possible. She pushed the car faster and headed for the highway.

Chapter 6
Tabby

Tabby stared out the window of the restaurant she was working in for the day. It had been two months since she'd seen the angel and werewolf fighting, and had started running. Her life had changed drastically since that day. Tabby had learned that to stay alive she needed to constantly keep running. She only stayed in one place about two days before she was off again.

She now drove a clunker she bought off someone for a case of beer. It got her from one place to another, but it was on it's last legs. She figured she'd drive it until it stopped, then she'd see if she could find another one. Wrecks were easy to find, and as long as she had a hundred bucks, she could get one without anyone finding out her name.

Tabby easily picked up work too. She could pretty much work in any bar or diner for a day and get paid in cash. Early on, she figured out that if she told people she was running from an abusive ex they would do more for her. She got free meals, she sometimes got places to stay, and she always got work. No one questioned her, but she probably looked like a crazy lady. She was always scanning where she was and looking for anyone that might be following her.

She'd learned a few tricks too. She was in a bar working one night when a werewolf walked in. He saw her from across the room and started to head her way. She quickly dumped her tray and headed in the back to get her purse. One of the waitresses was startled when she walked in and accidentally sprayed her with perfume.

Surprisingly, she had to pass the werewolf to get out. She made sure to keep to the shadows as she snuck past him, but she knew he'd eventually smell her. She was completely prepared to run, but the werewolf didn't even turn in her direction. Apparently, the perfume messed up his nose and masked her smell. Now, no matter where she was, she carried a bottle of the cheapest stuff she could buy in her pocket.

Tabby found werewolves and angels weren't the only paranormals after her. She had a vampire tailing her that first week. He was really hard to shake, but she found pitting paranormals against each other always worked. When one was after her she'd find another, and tell him the first one was after her. The second one would always kill the first one so he could have her for himself. Of course, she ran again while that was happening. Paranormals always figured she would be too scared to run, and that she would still be there when they got back.

She never did see Killian again, but she had seen the second angel twice more. Right after she ran she headed for New Orleans. It was probably a dumb idea, seeing as it's the paranormal capital of the world, but it's also the gathering place for many different witches.

Tabby visited several Wiccan and voodoo shops, and asked many questions. She finally found one of the most powerful witches around. Her name was Celeste, and once Tabby told her about her predicament, the witch was more than willing to help. Celeste gave her a crash course in everything supernatural, then loaded her up with tons of books. Tabby had been studying ever since. She looked for ways to hide from the different creatures, and found out what each creatures weakness was.

The witch had also taken Tabby to see another witch, who worked in a tattoo parlour. She had the second witch tattoo a sigil symbol on her ribs, just below her breasts. Apparently, the sigil was an ancient rune symbol that hid whoever wore it from angels. Tabby had cried after that and hugged both the witches. She had no other way to express her gratitude.

The witch also gave Tabby a necklace. It was basically a piece of ash, holly, and a green jasper crystal. They were wire wrapped together, and hung from a pretty velvet ribbon. The witch told her it would act as a ward against paranormals. Then she gave Tabby red and black cord to tie around her wrists. This also acted as a ward against paranormals.

The last thing she gave her was a ring that had a dzi bead in it. The dzi is an ancient agate relic from Tibet. Apparently, it acts as an eye, and would let her know when paranormals got near. She discovered quite quickly it warms up when they're close, proving the witch's claim.

Tabby spent two weeks with Celeste before leaving. She wouldn't put the witch's life in danger. But she definitely felt she would have been dead long ago, if not for her help.

She looked down now, as that same ring started to heat up. Before she could run the front door suddenly opened, and she gasped and then cursed as Killian walked in.

Chapter 7
Killian

Killian had been searching for Tabitha for months now, and he was tired of it. No matter what he did, or who he threatened, he seemed to stay just one step behind her. But that all changed today as he pushed the door to the diner open, and saw her standing behind the counter. He smirked at her, and she paled. Slowly, he stalked across the floor towards her.

He watched as she gulped once, then twice, then she turned and fled to the back. He heard a door slam, and cursed as he was forced to chase after her. He was too close to loose her now. Without slowing down, he held out his hands and pushed them forward, causing the door to open before he even reached it. He flew through it and saw she was just feet in front of him. She was trying to unlock her car door.

Killian slowed, and prowled towards her. Then he easily knocked the keys from her hand. He studied her, and saw she was trembling as she bent to retrieve the fallen keys. It bothered him that she was afraid of him. He grabbed her arm lightly and spun her to face him.

"Why are you afraid of me?" Killian curiously questioned.

"You're a death angel," she quietly answered. "And you've been chasing me for months. You're not supposed to be able to track me." Then she surprised him by lifting her shirt slightly and showing him the sigil symbol she had tattooed below her breast.

"This is supposed to hide me from you," she warily explained as she dropped her shirt to cover it again.

"Ah, Kitten," Killian purred. Then he watched as she frowned at the nickname and he smirked again. "Come on. Tabitha, Tabby, Kitten. You had to see that one coming." Her mouth dropped open in stunned silence, and he shook his head at her in agitation. "Fine," he grunted. "Now, the tattoo shields you from angels. I'm fallen Kitten, so it doesn't work on me."

"Damn," Killian heard her quietly whisper, and his lip turned up in a small smile. He pushed her to the side slightly, then bent and picked up her keys, slipping them in his pocket.

"You've been to a witch," he observed, as he took in the necklace and cords she had wrapped around her wrists.

"I've been to a witch," she immediately agreed. "But apparently, I need to go back," she complained to herself. She looked up in surprise as he chuckled.

"Kitten," Killian huffed in exasperation. "I'm not going to hurt you."

"Why not?" she questioned as she crossed her arms. "Everybody else is."

His back went ramrod straight at her declaration and his muscles tensed. "Who the hells after you?" he demanded.

She raised a brow and took a hesitant step away from him. "You don't know what you did to me?" she asked in apparent surprise.

"No," Killian growled. "But you better bloody well tell me," he demanded.

"You tell me first," Tabby countered with open curiosity. "Why are you Fallen? And what exactly does that mean?"

He stared at her. "It means you were destined to die that night in the alley. Unfortunately for me, you stirred something in me and I couldn't do it. My punishment for taking the scum that hurt you when it wasn't his time, was to have my wings stripped. I'm a fallen now Kitten, and I'll walk this earth for eternity."

Her eyes got wide and a tear fell down her cheek. "That happened because of me?" she asked weakly. "I'm so sorry."

Killian tilted his head and studied her. She actually shed a tear for him. No one had ever done that before.

"You won't hurt me," she declared with a raised brow.

He shook his head, " I won't hurt you," he instantly promised.

"But I will," a voice growled from behind them. They both turned at the same time and found a huge man standing there staring at them.

"This is my lucky day," he declared. "Not only will I get the little girl that can't die, but I'll get the angel that made her that way."

Then he stalked forward, and Killian pushed his Kitten behind him. Today was getting a hell of a lot more interesting, he thought, as he raised his hands and pushed at the air. It sent the man flying towards the wall. Bricks fell and the wall cracked, but the man just stepped forward and dusted himself off.

"Game on," he growled as they both charged each other.

Chapter 8
Tabby

Killian had hit the man hard and the wall had caved in, but the man just shook it off and kept coming. Tabby looked on in unease, unsure about how to help. Killian was strong, she knew that, but this man was stronger than any she'd encountered before.

"What is he?" she demanded as Killian hit the man again, forcing him against the wall a second time.

"Not sure, Kitten," Killian growled. "But I'll fucking find out." Then he ran at the man, and the crash of hard bodies clashing shook the ground.

Tabby hurried to the trunk of the car and patted her pockets, looking for the keys. When she couldn't find them she cursed Killian, forgetting for a minute he had taken them from her. She glanced back in his direction and froze on the spot.

The man fighting Killian had changed. His hair had disappeared completely, and not just the hair on top of his head, his eyebrows were gone and his arms looked completely smooth. His skin now took on the appearance of scales. They were light in colour, but it creeped Tabby out. His eyes were shaped like a snakes, and his teeth had turned wicked sharp. The man tried to snap at Killian as they fought, so Tabby figured now wasn't the time to request her keys back and distract him.

Tabby leaned down and pulled one of her small daggers from her boot. Then she crouched so she was eye level with the trunk lock. This was why she kept buying these old clunkers, they didn't have any electronic locks. If she lost her keys she could get in with a coat hanger, and start it up by twisting a couple wires.

Tabby shoved the dagger in the lock and twisted, wiggling it back and forth. When she turned back to Killian, she saw they were both on the ground now and the snake creature was on top. In Killian's defence though, the snake was bleeding from several places and looked worse for wear. He snapped at Killian with his teeth, and caught the fallen on his shoulder.

Killian roared and tried to pull the snakes head back, but without hair there was nothing to grab. Furiously, Killian punched the snake in the side of the head, but it didn't seem to do much. Blood now poured out of the fallen's shoulder and coated his shirt.

Tabby turned back to the lock and kept at it. A second later she heard the tell tale click of it opening, so she pulled out the dagger and ripped up the lid. She quickly undid the zipper on the large black leather bag she had hidden in there, and reached for a long beautiful sword. Pulling it out, she turned and ran towards the fight.

Killian was fighting with everything he had, but even though he had flipped them and was now on top, the teeth were still embedded in his shoulder. The snake was weakening quickly, but still he hung on.

"Get your head out of the way," Tabby screamed at him as she stopped beside them. Killian leaned to the side, exposing most of the snakes body. The minute he was out of the way she plunged the blade in the snakes chest.

The snake roared and reared back, instantly releasing Killian. Killian rolled out of the way and jumped to his feet. Even with the wound the man was incredible. Tabby turned her attention back to the snake, as he climbed to his feet and headed straight for her.

"You want to play little girl? Let's play," he hissed at her.

Shivers ran over her body from the sound of his voice. She took one step forward, then threw the sword over the beasts head, right at Killian. Killian quickly threw up an arm and snatched the thing right out of the air.

"The head," she screamed. "You take down a snake by cutting off its head." Then she jerked back as the snake made a lunge for her. It's nails scratched a bloody trail down her arm, but it didn't get a hold of her.

It reached again, but Killian was in position now. He drew back his arm and swung, taking off the head in one powerful go. Tabby stared wide eyed as the snakes head fell one way, and his body fell the other. Then it's eyes stared up at her unblinking, but the body still twitched. Killian stabbed it three more times for good measure, and finally the thing stilled. He then wiped the blade on the snakes shirt and crossed the area to stand in front of her.

"Fine," Tabby huffed as she placed her hands on her hips and looked up at him. "I guess you can stay with me."

Killian stared at her for a minute, then threw back his head and laughed.

Chapter 9
Killian

Killian climbed in the drivers seat of the clunker, and put the keys he had snatched from his kitten in the ignition. A quick flick of his wrist, and the car growled with life. He was actually surprised when the car started, he figured it was a fifty fifty crap shoot. He put his arm on the passenger seat, turned his head, and backed out. Moving down the lane he pulled on the main road and headed out. When he glanced at his kitten she was glaring at him.

"What's wrong now?" he sighed.

"It's my car, I should be driving it," Tabby huffed in obvious annoyance.

"Yeah, not happening," he told her. "You've been taking care of yourself for awhile now, and you've done well, but you won't be doing that anymore."

She blinked as she looked over at him.

"What does that mean?" she warily questioned.

"It means kitten, that you're my responsibility. And I take that seriously. I'm not fucking watching you die, and I'll do everything in my power to stop that from happening," Killian growled. "Plus, I kind of like that cute body of yours, and I'll be very upset if it doesn't stay that way," he added with a wink.

Killian chuckled when she chose to ignore that and gave him directions to where she was staying. It was a small two story apartment that looked like it might hold about six units. He pulled around back and parked where she directed him to. A minute later they were climbing the outside stairs to the second floor.

"Which apartment?" Killian inquired as they hit the landing. She turned her head slightly to answer as she continued walking.

"I'm the last apartment on the end. It gives me a better view of the street from two sides, and it gives me more options for escape," she explained.

Killian nodded in approval. "Smart," he told her.

"Glad you approve," Tabby mumbled as she held out her hands for the keys.

He ignored her, pushing past her and approaching the door first. He unlocked it and glared at her.

"Stay in the doorway and don't come in until I say it's okay," Killian ordered. His kitten saluted him, and he had to bite back his grin. Even after everything the poor girl had been through she still had some spunk.

He prowled through the tiny apartment and was surprised at how nice it was. The walls were a neutral beige, the furniture looked new and comfortable, and it appeared to be expensively decorated. He instantly frowned. It was horribly boring and it didn't suit her at all.

He made sure it was safe then headed back to the door. He was both surprised and happy to see she was leaning against the door jam, exactly where he left her.

"I figured you'd be halfway to China by now," Killian grunted with a raised brow.

"Don't think I didn't consider it," she replied as she stepped inside and shut the door.

"Nice place," he told her. "But it doesn't suit you."

"Thanks," she snickered. "Not good enough for it?" she questioned.

"Never," Killian denied. "It just seems too formal, not cozy and fun like I expect a place you live in to be." She smiled at him, and it looked beautiful on her.

"I'm apartment sitting for a regular at the diner. She's out of town on business for a week, and knew I needed a place to stay," she explained.

"Where do you normally stay?" he questioned.

"Cheap motels when I can afford it, my car when I can't," Tabby shrugged.

Killian growled at her answer, not liking it one bit. "You won't be sleeping in your car anymore kitten," he declared. "You'll be sleeping in a bed." Then he changed the subject before she could argue. "Your arm looks like it's bleeding pretty bad where he sliced you. We need to clean that up and bandage it. Snake shifters carry a lot of diseases, so the faster we get on that the better."

Tabby looked at him wide eyed. "He only scratched me," she whispered. "He sank his teeth into you. Besides, I'm a quick healer now, so it's no problem."

"I'm not taking any chances. And I'm a Fallen. I can't get an infection, and I'll still heal faster than you will," he informed her. "Bathroom now," he ordered as he pointed down the hall. "There's got to be some first aid supplies in there we can use."

She nodded and headed in that direction. Once there, she snagged the first aid kit from under the sink. He watched her as she got a look at her arm in the mirror and grimaced.

"I really hope it isn't as bad as it looks," she whispered.

"Snakes are dangerous creatures. Even the smallest injury can be bad," he honestly explained. "Take off your top so I can get a good look." She glared at him in the mirror, then reached up and tore the sleeve off.

"Well, that's no fun," Killian frowned. Then he shifted her sideways and got to work.

Chapter 10
Tabby

Tabby studied Killian as he cleaned her wound. For a fallen angel he seemed extremely relaxed. He took his time and worked carefully. His touch was actually warm, and she secretly enjoyed it.

"So, what's changed since you fell?" she asked. "From the way you handled that snake thing, I'd say your strength is equivalent to super man."

Killian chuckled at that. "Nothing much has changed. Of course I don't have my wings anymore, so flying is out, but I have retained all my other abilities," he patiently told her.

"Like what?" she pushed with a raised brow.

He put down the antiseptic and smirked at her. "Well, Kitten, you're going to have to stick around for a while if you want to learn my secrets."

She frowned at that. "I don't really have much of a choice now, do I."

"No, you don't," he confirmed as he wrapped her injury in gauze.

"Why didn't you take me that night?" she suddenly questioned.

She watched as he put away the supplies, effectively letting her know she wasn't looking at his wound. Then backed up. He leaned against the opposite wall and crossed his arms, causing her to shiver. It felt he was looking right through her as he studied her.

"I have no idea," Killian admitted. "I was prepared to take you." He titled his head and his eyes bore into her. "Something about you stopped me."

"What?" she curiously whispered.

"I don't know," Killian answered with a frown. "You reached out to me, and you called to me. You shouldn't have been able to see me."

"So, it's because of that?" Tabby asked.

"No," he admitted, confusing her more. "I've never felt before," Killian continued. "When I saw you, I experienced feelings I've never even known exist." He paused then and moved to lean against the counter beside her.

"I felt sad for what I was about to do. I felt anger at the man for hurting you. I felt pain for what you were experiencing. But, I also felt a connection with you. It was almost as if your soul called out to me," he explained.

"So you think we're soul mates?" Tabby whispered.

"I don't know," Killian frowned. "But, I intend to find out. For some reason your injuries healed, and I've never seen that before. I'm assuming a lot of paranormals are going to want their hands on you."

"Yeah," Tabby chuckled. "I've noticed that. So, what do we do to stop them from wanting me?" she asked.

"I have no idea, but I'm gonna find out," Killian growled. "I'm not the only fallen. Someone's got to know what the hell's going on with you."

"So how did you find me?" she questioned, deciding a change of topic was needed.

"I've been tracking you for a while," Killian grinned. "But you move fast and I couldn't get a lock on you until now. I can always sense the area your in, and the longer I've been hunting you, the better that little sense has become."

"So, others can sense me too?" Tabby asked with a small amount of fear.

"Maybe," he grunted with a shrug.

"So, can others sense you?" she continued. "Because if that's the case, you'll lead every paranormal right to me."

Killian frowned then. "Things are different for angels. Most paranormal can't sense them, and even though I'm fallen, that should still ring true. But, if for some reason they can, most won't be able to figure out what I am. That's going to work in our favour."

"How?" she immediately questioned.

"Because they'll underestimate me," Killian smirked. "Fallen are one of the strongest paranormals there are."

"So, can I die?" Tabby asked softly.

Killian reached out and brushed the hair off her face. "That's what I intend to find out. I touched you when it was your time, but it didn't kill you. Although, usually I don't touch my intended until after they pass. That could be it, or it could be something as simple as the fact that your time never came, and now it can't," he replied. "I've never heard of a case such as yours before."

"So now what?" she sighed.

"We get some sleep and then go find ourselves a fallen. There's a bar not too far from here I know for a fact one hangs out in. He used to be a friend," Killian admitted.

"And if he's not now?" Tabby warily asked.

"Then things are about to get even more interesting," he smirked.

Chapter 11
Killian

Killian tossed and turned on the tiny chesterfield he had been ordered to sleep on. His huge body hung over the sides and end, and he was sure he looked ridiculous. The flowery pillow and tiny blanket did nothing to help the look. He sighed and tried to roll over, but his elbow smashed into the coffee table, and it hurt like hell.

Growling, he pushed off the stupid thing and threw the blanket to the floor. He headed for the patio doors and made his way outside to stand on the balcony. The cool air and dark sky instantly calmed him. He wanted nothing more than to take to sky, and the itch to do so burned him inside.

Killian hated that Azriel had taken his wings. He knew the angel was only doing his job, but he had considered him a close friend. He could still feel a dull throbbing in his back where his wings has once rested, and he had a feeling that ache would never go away.

He then thought of the girl asleep inside the apartment. He had been astonished with the things she had accomplished since he had left her. The fact that she had consulted with a witch was an incredibly smart thing to do. He knew without a doubt, the items the witch had provided her with were helping her.

And then there was the fact she was studying the paranormals that were after her. She had an arsenal in her trunk, and she knew how to use each weapon. She had been helpful when he had battled the snake creature.

Killian had been shocked though, when she hadn't bolted during the fight. He had assumed as soon as he was distracted, she'd disappear. He had been pleasantly surprised when she pulled the sword and entered the fight. Unfortunately, that only endeared him towards her more.

Suddenly, his back went straight, and he had a feeling he was being watched. Killian moved closer to the shadows of the building and scanned the street below. Immediately, his eyes landed on the figure lazing against a lamp post, where unsurprisingly the bulb had been broken. He chuckled as he leaped over the railing and dropped two stories, to land on his feet far below.

Killian prowled across the street as the wolf pushed off the lamp post and met him halfway. They half hugged and pounded each other violently on the back.

"Cade, what brings you to my door?" Killian questioned with a grin. "And how the fuck did you find me?"

Killian had met Cade years ago. The enforcer had been in a battle, and things weren't looking good. Killian had been there for his attacker, but somehow the tables had turned on

Cade. Killian had immediately stepped in and taken the other wolf out. He had allowed Cade to see him then, and the wolf still felt he owed him.

"There's word spreading among the packs there's a girl that can't die. Apparently, she was touched by an angel and her blood contains the secrets to eternal life," Cade scoffed.

Killian's back went ramrod straight. "All the packs are aware of her," Killian asked.

Cade gave a quick nod. "Thought you needed a heads up."

"Tabby told me a wolf came after her," Killian told the Enforcer.

"Well, expect more. Word spreads quickly through the packs. The enforcers and council are trying to explain that her blood will do nothing for our kind, but I have a feeling the wolves who take you on will want to see that for themselves," Cade grunted.

"Wonderful," Killian snickered. "Wolf bites burn like a mother fucker."

Cade snorted. "Baby."

Killian flipped him off. "You never said how you found me."

"I followed a rogue here. His body's in the alley around the corner. I know your scent now, and I recognized it immediately. Figure he was here for the girl," Cade informed him. "I needed to tell you about the trouble coming for your girl anyway, so two birds with one stone."

Killian grinned. "Right. Surprised you left Tansi and your son alone."

"James is visiting with Piper and his new little girl. She's protected, and I knew I wouldn't be gone long," Cade grinned.

Killian appreciated the heads up. "You heading back now?"

"Yep," Cade confirmed. "I don't like to be away long." Then he turned and strode away, disappearing into the night.

Killian headed back to the apartment. With a powerful leap he was standing on the balcony once more. He hoped like hell his Kitten had a ton of silver bullets, because it looked like they were going to need them.

Chapter 12
Tabby

Tabby woke slowly. She was lying on her stomach and the bed was harder than she remembered. She peeped out from half closed eyes, and screamed blue murder when she saw a pair of eyes staring back at her. Instinctively, she raised her first and punched.

When Killian roared and sat up she was thrown from his chest, and found herself hanging off the end of the bed. She flailed for a minute, until the front of her shirt was grabbed and she was hauled back. Once more she found herself staring into Killian's eyes. One of his eyes was a deep shade of red, and it looked like it was already bruising. Curiously, she poked at it.

"Jesus," Killian cursed as he knocked her hand away. "You don't need to poke it."

"You can bruise," Tabby responded in awe.

He ignored her. "You always punch your bed partners?" he growled.

"I do if they weren't invited," she growled back. "I told you to sleep on the couch."

"Look at me, Kitten. I didn't fucking fit on the couch. Besides that, you were sleeping on a third of the bed, it was a waste," Killian shrugged.

"Well, why did you pull me on top of you then?" Tabby asked.

"I got cold," he smirked. Her mouth dropped open and she would have said something, but he was faster.

"Get up. I got word last night that your ability to heal has spread through all the wolf packs. Apparently, we may be getting visitors soon," Killian told her.

Tabby immediately jumped off the bed and scrambled for her clothes. She headed for the bathroom and ran the shower as her mind raced. One wolf she could handle, but several, she didn't think she'd survive. She hurried through her morning routine, then towel dried her hair. The sun could dry the rest of it. Twenty minutes later she was back and motioning for Killian to take his turn.

She knew Killian wanted to find his friend, and she knew her time here was up. She packed up her things as she sadly looked around the space. She had actually felt normal for a bit, working in the restaurant and staying here.

Killian eyed her as soon as he came out of the bathroom. "What's wrong?" he demanded.

"I'm sad it's time to go. I was comfortable here," Tabby admitted.

"You'll find a way to be comfortable again, but it may be a while before that happens. Your life has changed, your going to have to learn to accept the new you," he advised.

"So, this is me now. There's no fixing this?" Tabby frowned.

Killian nodded, and she knew he didn't want to sugar coat it for her. She sighed and turned to the door when Killian suddenly clamped his hand down on her shoulder. When she turned to look at him curiously, he put a finger to his mouth, signalling her to be quiet. Her body instantly went on alert.

Killian pulled her towards the balcony doors and she followed him without question. When a crash sounded at the front door, and the wood started to splinter, Killian picked her up and ran for the patio. He kicked out with his booted foot and the doors opened, then he was hurrying to the rail. She stared up at him in horror.

"Don't even think about it," Tabby growled. "I'm learning how to fight. We can take them together."

When he ignored her and leaped over the railing she closed her eyes and screamed. The fall was quick, and with the way he tucked her body into his chest, she wasn't even jarred. He dropped her to her feet and they both ran for her clunker. When they reached it, he opened the drivers side and pushed her across the seat, then climbed in after her.

The ground shook and she looked back to see three large wolves had dropped from the apartment above.

"Go," she yelled at Killian.

Suddenly the car raced forward, but one of the wolves leaped and landed on the trunk of their car. Claws punched through the glass and Killian swore.

Tabby calmly leaned over and searched the floor under the drivers seat. When her hand touched what she was looking for, she yanked it out and pulled back the hammer. Then she fired at the wolf. The wolf howled as the bullet tore through it's shoulder. Then she watched as it lost its grip and rolled down the road.

"You got any more surprises hidden under my seat that you need to reach for?" Killian smirked.

Tabby couldn't help it, the wolves had all been left behind and they had gotten away. She turned to Killian and grinned.

Chapter 13
Killian

Killian glanced at his kitten, then turned back to the road. She had fallen asleep two hours into the drive. He knew she must be exhausted. For months she had been on her own with no one to watch her back. She would have needed to be alert constantly, and it appeared that had taken a toll on her body.

By falling asleep she had just put her complete trust in him. She had allowed herself to be vulnerable, and he took that seriously. It meant a lot to him that she trusted him. He wanted to make her his completely, but he knew he had to move slowly. He couldn't afford to scare her off.

Killian drove for another six hours, before he decided she needed food. He knew he needed it too, and it irritated him. Angels never stopped to ea. It wasn't necessary, but as a fallen his body demanded food. He could only push himself so long until odd noises came from his stomach.

He saw a truck stop up ahead and immediately slowed the car to take the turn off. He pulled up to a set of pumps and turned the car off. Deciding to let his Kitten wake on her own he stepped out and topped up the tank. After paying he climbed back in, happy to see she was waking up.

"Where are we?" she asked groggily.

"Not too far from where we're headed, but you need food," Killian told her as he started the car up and headed for the parking lot. A minute later he was out and opening her door for her.

"Come on Kitten. You can sleep again after," he smirked.

Killian held out his hand and was pleased when she took it. He maneuvered her through the lot and held the door for her as she went inside. He easily moved through the restaurant and chose a table near the back, but one that was beside a window. He could see everyone that came in the door, but it would be harder for them to see him. Plus, it had a clear view of the lot.

"Good choice," his Kitten approved, taking him by surprise. She slid into the seat across from him and picked up the menu. He smiled as he did the same.

A minute later a waitress came up to the table. She had her head down as she pulled out a pen and pencil.

"What can I get you," she questioned with impatience. Then she frowned when neither of them answered. She looked up and noticed him, then immediately perked up. She leaned on the table so her cleavage showed and completely ignored his girl.

"Well, honey, it's nice to see a real man in these parts. You see anything you like?" she purred.

Killian caught his Kitten glaring at the woman out of the corner of his eye. He smiled at the waitress, then gave his full attention to Tabby.

"I do, but she's playing hard to get," he announced. "You have any suggestions?"

The waitress immediately stood up and tapped her foot. "The menu?" she amended with a glare.

"Oh, sorry, bring me two breakfast specials and two glasses of orange juice," Killian told her.

She nodded, but before she turned away she got in her two cents.

"You could do so much better than her," she purred. Then she ripped off a slip of paper and slid it to him. Before he could respond she was gone. He looked down to see a name and number on it.

"Thanks," his Kitten frowned sarcastically. "By defending my honour you just gave her a reason to spit in my food."

"What?" he questioned, not understanding.

"You should have said nothing. She obviously likes you, and you outright told her she didn't have a shot. She'll take that out on my food," Tabby sadly explained.

Killian watched his Kitten, and waited until the waitress came back with their food. Not once did she look up, and when the food was placed before her, she didn't even make a move to touch it. Before the waitress left, Killian moved quickly and switched the plates.

"Your plate looks like it has more food, and I'm starving," he shrugged when she looked up at him in surprise. He grabbed his fork and was about to dig in, when his plate suddenly disappeared.

"So sorry, I'm sure I saw a bug. Let me just get you a new one," the waitress apologized. Then she was gone.

"Thank you," Tabby whispered as she sighed. Then she pushed the plate in the middle of the table. "We can share until she comes back."

Killian smiled, then picked up a piece of bacon. His Kitten was falling for him, and she didn't even know it.

Chapter 14
Tabby

Tabby was thrilled when Killian decided to stop for the night. She'd had enough of the car and she couldn't wait to stretch her legs. The motel he picked certainly didn't look like much, but right now she couldn't care less. As soon as he stopped she threw open the door and climbed out.

"Jesus," she complained. "I thought you were never going to stop."

Tabby heard him chuckle, but she ignored him as she started doing laps around the car. She was stiff and she needed to move. She circled around him as he grabbed her knapsack and headed for the front office. Sighing, she stopped and followed him.

When he stepped inside she was right on his heels. The office was small, but she was beyond happy to see it was surprisingly clean. He stood and waited patiently, but she hurried over and tapped the bell on the counter twice.

"You're going stand there all day," Tabby complained when he raised his eyebrow in question.

After a minute an older man came out of a small door, and smiled when he saw them. He made his way to the counter just as Killian leaned against it.

"Well hello," he greeted. "You youngsters need a room for the night?"

"We need two please," Tabby immediately informed him.

"Now Kitten," Killian immediately sighed as he tagged her hand and pulled her into his side. "You going to leave me all alone on our wedding night?"

Tabby frowned at him and poked him as hard as she could in his ribs. Of course, the ass didn't even twitch.

"You're newlyweds," the old man cried as he clapped his hands and lit up like a Christmas tree. "I've got just the room for you. It's the last one on the end and it's pretty quiet. There's only a few guests and they're spread out pretty good."

"That sounds perfect," Killian agreed as he smirked down at her. "I can't wait to get some alone time with my girl."

"Awww, you two are adorable. Just fill out this card and we'll get you on your way," the old man requested as he pushed a pen towards them.

Tabby used that as her excuse, and pulled away from Killian. She signed it with a fake name, then handed over some cash.

"Enjoy your stay," the motel owner told them as he handed Killian a key. The ass saluted the old man, then dragged her out the door.

"Why the hell do we need to share a room?" Tabby complained as they crossed the parking lot.

"Because you've got every paranormal in the universe after you Kitten," Killian answered. "And I'm going to be there to stop them."

"I've done just fine on my own," she told him as she threw her hands up in the air. "I'm still in one piece."

"You are," Killian agreed as his eyes traveled up and down her body. "But your luck can't last forever, and as much as I admire what you've done so far, I'm here now to help."

He then unlocked the door to the room and Tabby followed him inside. When Killian threw her bag on the bed she immediately grabbed it. She searched inside, grabbed the box she wanted, and headed for the window. In seconds she had a thick, even line of salt drawn along the edge.

"What the hell are you doing?" Killian questioned as she headed for the door. She crouched down and drew another line at the bottom.

"Keeping out demons and ghosts," she explained. "I'm not taking any chances." She peeked in the bathroom, but it didn't have any windows.

Tabby moved to her bag, shoved the box of salt back inside, then grabbed clean clothes.

"I'm showering first. I won't be long," she promised.

"We could shower together to save time," Killian responded.

Tabby practically ran through the door, slammed it shut and locked it, before her stupid mouth could say yes. She really liked Killian, but she wasn't ready for that yet. She hurried through her shower then watched as Killian went in to take his turn.

While he was gone she took all the extra pillows and made a pillow fort down the middle of the bed. When he came out he stopped cold.

"Is that a pillow wall?" the ass chuckled.

"It is. You stay on your side and I'll stay on mine," she ordered, which only made him laugh harder as he climbed in.

Tabby fell asleep knowing she was safe for the night, both from him, and from everything else.

Chapter 15
Killian

Killian woke to find his Kitten sprawled across his chest. He smirked, knowing sometime during the night she must have destroyed her pillow wall. She obviously liked him. She was just trying to fight it and he could understand that. The poor girl had enough things going on in her life, she probably didn't need him added into the mix.

He stroked her thick, beautiful hair, and watched as she started to wake. He knew the minute she was, because her whole body locked solid.

"I climbed over the pillow fort, didn't I?" she whispered.

Killian smirked. "You did, but it was a valiant effort on your part."

Tabby suddenly smacked his chest and he grunted in surprise. "You could have resisted at least a little bit," she complained.

"No fucking way," he growled. "You're exactly where I want you to be. Your stupid pillow wall was a waste of time."

"It was not," Tabby argued, but he'd heard enough. He grabbed the back of her neck and dragged her down as he crashed his mouth against hers. She didn't move a muscle, and Killian thought for sure she would push him away, but then she relaxed. Her arms went around him, her weight dropped on his, and her mouth softened.

Killian kissed her long and deep, until he had to let go and breathe. When he pulled back she looked completely stunned.

"You're good at that," Tabby whispered, then promptly slapped her hand over her mouth.

Killian chuckled as a blush crept across her chest and cheeks. He brushed her hair out of her eyes, then tapped her bottom.

"Looks like your salt trick worked Kitten. It was an unusually quiet night," he grinned.

She grinned back as she pushed off him and rolled off the bed. She grabbed the box, brushed as much as she could back into it, and shoved it in her bag.

"Smart girl," Killian complimented as he watched her grab some clothes and head into the bathroom. He dressed too while he waited for her. When they were both ready, they headed out.

Killian stopped short when he saw her poor car. All the tires were flat, the windows were shattered, and the hood was up. It looked like every part of the engine was now laying on the pavement beside it.

"Was that necessary?" Killian questioned the vampire that was sitting on the car's roof. At the same time, he pushed his Kitten behind him. He heard her rummaging through her knapsack, but he ignored her.

"I tried to be patient, but I got bored. It's still early, but the suns coming up soon and I'm running out of time and patience," the vampire shrugged.

"Is this the one that was after you?" he asked Tabby.

She peered around him, then stuck her head back in her bag. "Nope, this is a new guy."

As he watched, the vampire suddenly jumped from the hood and sailed towards them. Killian pushed Tabby out of the way as the vampire's body crashed into his. Killian hauled back and punched him as he ducked, trying to stay away from the creature's teeth.

The vampire's head rocked back, then he snarled at Killian, revealing the two long fangs. Killian charged him again, taking them both to the ground. The vampire shoved his sharp nails into Killian's side causing him to roar in pain. He grabbed the creature's head and slammed it against the cement over and over, until the creature finally went limp.

When Killian moved off, he turned to see Tabby crying out at him. He whipped his head back to the vampire, but it was too late. The vampire grabbed the neck of his shirt and flung him across the parking lot. Before he could even stand the vampire had Tabby in a tight embrace, and his fangs were inches from her neck.

"I'm going to enjoy tasting you," the vampire salivated. He lowered his head and Killian tore across the lot, knowing he wouldn't reach them in time.

When the vampire screamed, Killian didn't stop. He ripped his Kitten away from the creature and shoved him into the side of the motel. Wood splintered and gave way as the vampire fell into the room they just left.

Killian stepped through the opening and stared down at the bloody, smoking mess that was now the creatures face. When he looked back at his girl she was holding a squirt gun.

"Holy water," she grinned in explanation as she tilted her head. "Very affective."

Killian ignored her as he placed his hands together and concentrated. When they heated enough that sparks flew out from between them, he pulled them apart and turned his palms towards the vampire. A massive ball of fire shot out from them and hit the vampire in the chest. In seconds the vampire was no more than a pile of ash.

Tabby looked at her water gun, then looked at his hands. "Is this one of those things you told me I'd find out as I go?" she asked.

He reached for her hand and she jumped back, knocking his away.

Killian huffed as he glared at her. "I'd never fucking hurt you," he growled in agitation. "As soon as the fire's released they cool again."

Tabby stepped closer and jabbed her pinky into his palm quickly. When she wasn't burned, she smiled.

"That's cool," she grinned as she grabbed his hand fully and dragged him away.

Chapter 16
Tabby

"Quit staring at my hands," Killian growled as he drove down the road. They had retrieved her stash of weapons from the trunk and had deposited them in another car Killian had claimed he borrowed. And the jerk had smirked when he said it. She immediately knew borrowed meant he stole the damn thing.

"Your hands fascinate me now," Tabby admitted with a half shrug. She was in awe of what he could do, and she couldn't wait to discover what else he had hidden in his bag of tricks.

"They can do a lot of things," Killian purred as he grinned at her. "You want me to pull over and show you."

"No I do not," she outright lied. "So, how did you become an angel? Or were you born that way?"

"No Kitten," Killian smirked. "No angels are born. We all become angels after our deaths. I was a soldier in the Trojan war in 12th century BC."

Her jaw dropped open and she stared at him in shock. "That war is only a legend. It was a Greek myth," she chocked out.

"All legends are based on historical events. Look at King Arthur and Noah's Ark. You do know they discovered the Ark?" Killian questioned.

"I'd heard that," Tabby admitted. "But the Trojan War, that's just crazy."

"It's not," Killian denied with a hard expression. "I was part of the Trojan soldiers that defended Troy from the Achaeans. The siege itself lasted ten years, and many great soldiers were killed. I considered them good friends. The city fell when the Trojan horse got through the gates."

"The Trojan horse was a real thing?" she asked in complete surprise.

"It was, and it was our downfall. Everyone left was slaughtered or kept as slaves. They desecrated our temples and in doing so earned the gods wrath," he patiently explained.

"Where was Troy?" Tabby questioned curiously.

"It was in the country of Turkey," Killian imparted.

"So you died in the war?" she asked as she turned completely in her seat to look at him.

"I was one of the last soldiers to be killed," he smirked at her.

"Of course you were," Tabby grinned, trying to picture him in leather and wearing metal armour. She could see him in one of those ridiculous helmets with the feathery looking Mohawks sticking out of the top, and brandishing a sword.

"So, that's why you were so good with the sword when the snake thing attacked us?" she inquired.

"The sword is like a third arm to me," Killian admitted. "I feel lost without it."

"I'm sorry," Tabby sighed. "How did you die?"

"Twelve soldiers descended on me at once, as I said, there weren't many of us left. Ten I could take on, twelve I could not. I ran three through with my sword before one of there's pierced my armour and drove through my chest," he huffed.

"And you woke up an angel?" she assumed.

"No," Killian denied. "I woke to find a man with wings standing over me. He gave me a choice. I could rest in peace with my fallen brothers, or I could go with him and become something more. I didn't want to die," he admitted.

"So, you got to pick what kind of angel you wanted to be, or you were just assigned one," she pushed.

"We don't get a choice. Apparently, they were waiting for me to die. My fate had already been sealed," he growled.

"So, what about me?" she hedged with a frown. "If our fate's already sealed and I didn't die, what happens now?"

"That's what I need to figure out," he growled. "There's a reason you can't die, and there's a reason all the paranormals are hunting you. I'm hoping my friend can get us some answers."

Then something else occurred to her, and she turned in her seat to face him. "So you're over 3000 years old," she teased. "You're way too old for me and far too experienced. I can imagine a soldier of Troy had a lot of woman pawing at him."

Killian turned to her and grinned. "I had a lot of bed partners," he easily agreed. "But think of all the experience I've had."

Tabby frowned at him as he conveniently turned the tables on her. "I don't really want to think about that," she pouted.

"Okay, then think of the fact that I've been an angel for that long as well. Angels don't have feelings and they certainly don't have sex. I've also been celibate for 3000 years Kitten," he growled.

"Jesus," she whispered as heat creeped over her face. "That's a long time."

"When we get together, I can guarantee its going to be explosive," he smirked.

Tabby crossed her legs and turned back to the window. "I'm suddenly tired," she fake yawned. "I think I'll go back to sleep."

Killian threw back his head and laughed, and she blushed even more.

Chapter 17
Killian

Killian pulled up to the bar where he hoped to find Mace and shut off the engine. When he had stopped to buy his kitten some dinner, she casually declared she needed to use the bathroom to change. The minute she stepped back out the fighting had started, and it hadn't stopped since. She came out with her hair teased, makeup on, wearing jeans that looked painted on, and a loose off the shoulder top that showed way too much skin. The icing on the cake though, were the shoes.

"What the fuck's on your feet?" he yelled a minute after he had dragged her out into the parking lot.

"Ummm, shoes," she answered with a raised brow.

"Those aren't shoes," Killian had roared. "Those are high heels, and is that a leopard pattern on them?"

Tabby had actually giggled then, which only pissed him off more. "You call me kitten. I thought they were fitting."

His mouth dropped open, then he shut it and glared at her. "Change them, and that outfit while you're at it."

She pushed past him and got in the car, refusing to look at him. Killian had no choice but to stalk around to the drivers side and throw himself in if he wanted to continue this conversation.

"Where the fuck did you get that outfit anyway?" he demanded.

"It's my emergency outfit," she declared. "And it doesn't actually take up a lot of room."

"I can see that," he growled. "I can also see a lot of skin."

"We're going to a club," Tabby whispered in a shock voice. "I need to fit in."

"You'll never fit in," Killian declared. "You stand out no matter where you go."

She had no reply to that, so she turned and conveniently stared out the window. He couldn't help but chuckle at her.

That brought them to now, and Killian knew it was time to get out and go look for Mace. When he turned to Tabby, she was pale and shaking. Immediately he tensed, not liking the fear he could see in her eyes.

"What's wrong?" he demanded.

Tabby didn't look at him, but continued to stare out the window. "The last time I was at a bar, I went looking for my father. He was drunk again and I had to pick him up. I never made it because I was attacked in the alley. It was the night I met you," she softly explained to him.

Killian moved quickly, snagging her around the waist and dragging her across the car so she was sitting in his lap. She squeaked, then looked up at him in confusion.

"I saved you that night, and I'll do it again. You're absolutely safe with me. And anyone that thinks to mess with you, will have to go through me." He smirked then, causing her to blink up at him. "And Kitten, I'm not easy to go through."

She just stared at him wide eyed, so he continued. "I'm sorry you never got to your dad that night. I promise that when this ends, we'll go back and let him know you're safe."

Tabby frowned at him. "My whole life my dad has been a drunk. My mom left when I was so small, I don't remember her. I've always had to take care of him, and I'm tired of it. I feed him. I clean his house. And, I usually pay his bar tabs when I'm called to get him. I can't do it anymore. I hate to say it, but it won't be the end of the world if I don't ever see him again."

Killian looked at her in anger. "Well I hope to see him again one day. I'm sure I could come up with a few things to say to him."

She grinned then. "Right, I've seen how you talk to people. It usually ends up in blood shed."

He sighed and couldn't argue that. "Let's go find Mace. I'm hoping he can help me figure things out."

"Mace?" she questioned. "Your friend's named Mace."

"Yeah," he grunted. "Why?"

"Killian, Cade, now Mace. You guys have some really badass names," she told him.

Killian smirked. "I'll take that as a compliment."

Tabby huffed and pushed off his lap, heading back to her side. Killian immediately jumped out and hurried around to her side with her leather jacket in his hands.

"Please Kitten," he begged. "Wear the jacket. I need to concentrate on getting us in there safely, finding Mace, and getting us back out. With you in that outfit, I'm going to have to fight off half the men in there as well. Have a bit of sympathy for me."

She smiled, and thankfully grabbed the jacket, surprising him. "Fine" she frowned. "But only because I have the pockets loaded up with knives and squirt guns filled with holy water."

Killian threw back his head and laughed. His girl was ready for anything, and he loved that about her.

Chapter 18
Killian

Killian felt on edge the minute he stepped into the dark bar. The floor was coated in sticky beer, the lighting was low, and the place was packed. He tensed when swaying bodies pressed against him as he pushed through the crowd and headed for the bar. He reached back and claimed his Kitten's small hand, pulling her body flush into the back of his.

"What are you doing?" she yelled up at him as she unsuccessfully tried to pull her hand free.

"I'm making sure I don't lose you in this fucking place," he growled as he turned and looked down at her.

"And you need me plastered to your back to ensure that?" Tabby questioned with a raised brow.

"Yes," Killian yelled back with barely restrained patience. "I sense a shit ton of immortals in this dive, and once they realize who you are, they'll all want a piece of you."

"I have my water gun," she ridiculously reminded him.

"Well be prepared to use it while you stay close to my back," he ordered in response.

Then he turned away, pulled her against him once more, and continued to shoulder his way through the crowd. There was absolutely no way he was letting her get even a foot away from him. He sensed werewolves, vampires, witches, and he even felt a phoenix was close by. He wasn't in the mood to test his powers against that one.

Killian finally reached the bar and stepped to the side so he could put Tabby in front of him. Once she was exactly where he wanted her he caged her in with his arms and leaned forward. His body now completely hid her small frame from almost the entire bar. With a quick whistle he caught the bartenders eye. The man immediately made his way over to them.

"Fallen," the man greeted. "What can I do for you?"

"Mace in tonight," Killian inquired as he ignored the Fallen comment. If the bartender knew Mace well, he'd be able to recognize another of his kind easily.

"He is. He actually took a pretty little wolf upstairs about an hour ago. He should be back down shortly. You want a drink while you wait?" he asked.

"Beer," Killian told him. "And a water for the lady."

"Whisky, neat", Tabby annoyingly shouted as she twisted and glared up at him. He rolled his eyes then nodded at the bartender.

"Make that two." When she smirked up at him in triumph he turned the glare on her. "You better be able to hold your liquor darling. I was hoping to be in and out, but it looks like this isn't going to be that easy."

"So maybe we should just go up and get him," Tabby suggested.

Killian couldn't help grinning down at her. "You want to walk in on him, be my guest. I'd be extremely unhappy if someone interrupted me. You don't want to make a Fallen angry, trust me on that Kitten."

"So we sit here and wait?" she asked with a scowl on her pretty face.

"We certainly aren't waiting long. Your safety is my priority, and we're sitting ducks just standing here," Killian told her. "I'll give him ten, then I'm moving."

The bartender reappeared and set two glasses down in front of them. Killian nodded his thanks and threw some bills down. The bartender grabbed them, nodded in thanks, and moved down the bar. Killian pushed a glass in front of Tabby and picked up the other one himself. He downed it in one gulp and slammed the empty glass upside down on the bar.

"I'm not carrying you out of here big guy, you better know how to hold your liquor," Tabby grunted, throwing his own words back at him.

He grinned down at her and watched as she took a sip of hers. Her nose scrunched up and her eyes watered.

"Good?" he asked with a smirk, swallowing his laugh. It was painfully obvious this was her first taste of whiskey.

"Yep," Tabby sputtered, struggling not to show the affect the drink was having on her.

He nodded at the bartender as he tipped his head down to indicate Tabby. The man looked at Tabby, shook his head, and came over with a bottle of water.

"Sorry, must be a bad batch," the bartender apologized as he removed her glass and replaced it with the water.

She nodded up at him like she agreed completely and drank half the bottle in one go.

"Okay badass, lets go up and find Mace," Killian ordered as he took her hand again and dragged her towards the stairs. When she swayed a bit, he couldn't help the chuckle that escaped.

Suddenly he was hit with a squirt of water in the ear. He swiped at the cold wetness running down the side of his face as he growled at her.

"Don't be a smart ass," she hissed. Then she grabbed his hand and started to pull him up the stairs, reversing their roles.

Killian would have laughed again, but she still held the damn water gun. She just kept surprising him. And he loved it.

Chapter 19
Tabby

Tabby reached the top of the stairs and stopped. There was no way she was opening that door and stepping into the room first. Killian seemed to trust Mace, but she didn't know him. With everyone out to kill her she wasn't taking any chances.

"What's the matter?" he muttered from where he was forced to stop behind her.

Tabby narrowed her eyes and glared up at him. "He's your friend. I think you should go first," she ordered as she stepped to the side.

Killian smirked, then raised his first and pounded on the door. Tabby heard muttered curse words from the other side, so without taking any chances she moved so she was mostly behind him.

Seconds later the door was thrown open and a massive looking giant was glaring back at them. He was handsome in a scary sort of way, and he was only wearing a pair of undone jeans.

"Who the fuck do you think you are, disturbing me?" the giant growled.

Killian chuckled and then shook his head. "Nice to see you again too Mace."

"Fuck, Killian," the giant grinned. "I heard you were banished down here, but I honestly didn't believe it."

Killian just shrugged and planted a hand on Mace's chest, shoving the giant back into the room. When he followed him in Tabby was right behind him. Killian promptly kicked the door shut behind them.

The first thing Tabby noticed was the girl who was desperately trying to do her dress up. She had it on okay, but the buttons were all messed up.

"I need to go," the girl whispered as she eyed them all. Mace immediately turned and prowled over to her. When he was close he tagged her behind the neck.

"You need me, you come to me," he all but growled. "You keep me posted of everything that's happening, and you don't run from me again."

She looked up at him, and Tabby swore she could see stars in the girls eyes. "Okay," she quietly agreed. Then she stood on tiptoes, kissed his cheek, and was gone. Tabby could only stare at the door as it seemed to open and shut again in a matter of seconds.

"She's cute," Killian stated, and both her and the giant turned furious eyes on him.

"Fuck off," Mace sneered as he did up his jeans and pulled a tee over his head.

"Hey, I've got a girl of my own. I'm not going after yours," Killian told the man as he pointed at her.

"I'm not your girl," Tabby immediately denied, but Killian simply rolled his eyes.

"Jesus you're a pain in my ass," he complained.

She completely ignored him and turned to the giant. "Is she going to be okay?" she questioned Mace.

"She will be," Mace responded angrily. "I'll make damn sure if it."

"I need your help," Killian interrupted, jumping right to the point of why they were there.

Mace raised an eyebrow and smirked at him. "There's a statement I've never heard from you before."

"Yeah well, there's a first time for everything," Killian scowled.

Mace gestured to both the bed and small table in the room. "Have a seat. I need a drink, but it's quieter up here."

As soon as Tabby headed for the bed Killian's hand shot out and caught her arm.

"I don't think so," he growled. Then he yanked her to the table, pushed her into a chair, dragged the other chair over so it was beside her, and sat down himself. Their thighs were touching he was so close.

Mace was chuckling when she looked up. "Never thought I'd see this. You're asking for help, and you're staking your claim on a girl."

"Can we get down to why we're here?" Killian asked angrily.

Mace raised his hands in surrender and motioned for Killian to continue.

"I was sent to take her soul. I flew into a situation I really didn't like, and I saved her instead. She was at deaths door. I dropped her at a hospital and miraculously she healed," Killian explained.

"So you didn't take a soul?" Mace questioned with a frown.

Killian huffed. "I did, it just wasn't hers. She was meant to die that day."

"So her injuries were life threatening?" Mace pushed, clearly wanting more information.

"She was barely breathing. Doctors these days are good, but not that good. She walked out of there hours later," Killian explained.

"So now she can't die," Mace deduced.

"Right, and every fucking paranormal wants a piece of her," Killian growled.

"So your wings were taken because you saved a soul you were supposed to take. And you took a soul you weren't supposed to take," Mace smirked.

Killian nodded and Mace laughed. "You're a dumb ass."

"Jesus," Killian grunted. "You're no help."

"You ever heard of the prophecy?" Mace asked, as his face turned serious and he leaned forward in his chair.

Tabby's heart started to beat fast in her chest, and she knew whatever he was going to say was going to be bad. But, before she could say a word an explosion shook the floor and horrible screams were heard from downstairs.

Chapter 20
Killian

Killian grabbed Tabby and pulled her to his chest as the floor began to shake from the force of the explosion below. Plaster from the ceiling rained down on them and items that had been on a dresser crashed to the floor. The minute the room settled Mace was out the door, and Killian moved to follow.

"Grab my belt loop and hold on. I want you close," Killian yelled back at his kitten.

As soon as he felt her fingers grip on, he hurried for the door. Unlike Mace, who had practically flown down the stairs, Killian was a bit more cautious. He had no idea what he would encounter, and he was in no hurray to walk into a setup. As they got closer to the bottom the dust made it almost impossible to see. Patrons were screaming, and some were bleeding, as they desperately made their way to the doors.

Killian stepped onto the floor of the main level and took a look around. It appeared the bomb had taken out the bar, so that was probably where it had been placed. He could just make out the body of the bartender sticking out from under some debris. It was clear from the blood and position of the body the man was dead.

He scanned again and located Mace in the middle of the wreckage. He was picking up broken tables and debris, and hurling them across the room. Killian moved to his side and grabbed his arm.

"What are you doing?" he questioned the Fallen.

"The little wolf I was with. I don't know if she made it out in time. I need to make sure she isn't buried in here somewhere," Mace growled as he continued digging.

Killian nodded, instantly knowing he'd do the same thing if it was his kitten. He motioned to her and she immediately let go, knowing that's what he wanted. She stuck close as he and Mace moved quickly and efficiently sifted through the debris.

They were almost done when the bar suddenly filled with vicious growling. Killian dropped the chair he was holding and turned to locate Tabby. She had moved with them while they worked, but right now she was closer to Mace. Both her and Mace were peering through the smoke, looking for the threat.

When huge creatures stepped out from every corner, Killian knew they were in trouble. He recognized right away that the wolves were rogue, and there was a good chance they were the ones Cade had warned him about. There were six of them, and the odds weren't good. He glanced at Tabby again, and saw she had pulled out a wicked looking silver knife. It was a good idea, but she'd have to get too close to the wolves to use it.

Furious that she was put in a position where she needed it, Killian stepped closer to the wolves and growled right back at them. The rogues had been staring at Tabby, but at his growl they spun around to face him. He glanced at Mace and made sure he had the Fallen's attention.

"The knife," he snarled as the wolves started to close in on them.

Mace understood immediately, and snatched the knife off Tabby before she even realized what he was doing. Then with a flick of his wrist, it was flying through the air. Killian reached up and snagged it, keeping his eyes on the advancing wolves.

"Get her out of here," he ordered just as the first wolf leapt.

Killian swung out with the knife and cut the wolves exposed belly as it took him down. They crashed to the floor, and Killian was quickly soaked with the wolves blood. He shoved up with everything he had and launched the gutted wolf across the room.

With only a second to spare until he was attacked again, Killian spun and watched as Mace caught a struggling Tabby around the waist. The Fallen wrapped his body around hers and leapt straight up into the air. His girl was screaming like a banshee as they crashed through the ceiling and landed on the second floor. Killian then heard the sound of breaking glass, and knew Mace had crashed through the window.

He turned back to the wolves, with his knife held high. When the wolves attacked as a group he was ready, knowing that Mace would look after his girl.

Chapter 21
Tabby

Tabby had fought Mace with everything she had, but it had no effect on the Fallen. Now she clung to him with her eyes squeezed tightly shut, and prayed Killian made it out alive.

The wolves had terrified her, and she knew something was wrong with them. They were mangy, they were thin, and they looked like they were foaming at the mouth. They reminded her of rabid dogs. Rogues. She had heard the term before, and she suddenly realized that was what they were.

Then Mace was grabbing her and they were crashing through the ceiling. Her body had been protected by his, but there had been enough time to watch one of the wolves leapt at Killian. Then Mace had jumped through a window, and they landed in the parking lot. Patrons were running, screaming and bleeding, and no one paid them any attention.

"Close your eyes tight and hold on," Mace had ordered. "If not, you'll end up throwing up all over me."

Then he had taken off at a speed she thought was reserved only for super heroes. The world tilted as the scenery blurred by at a dizzying rate. Immediately her stomach clenched, and she closed her eyes, understanding why he had told her to do so.

They ran for hours, until he finally started to slow. Carefully, she opened one eye and peered out. When her head didn't spin and the world went by at a much slower pace, she opened the other eye too. She was shocked at what she saw.

Everywhere Tabby looked were Cyprus trees, their trunks covered in twisting vines and moss. The ground was squishy, and every time Mace took a step, his foot sunk into the ground. She could hear frogs, and the mosquitoes were numerous. A thick mist gave everything a spooky quality, and it was so hot her clothes were instantly damp.

"Where are we?" she whispered to the Fallen.

Mace looked down at her and grinned. "We're deep in the swamp honey. It's the safest place I know of."

"The swamp," she gasped in surprise. "Killian will never find us here."

"Killian knows about this place. When it's safe for him, this is where he'll head," Mace patiently told her.

Then he stopped and lowered her feet to the ground. "You can walk the rest of the way," he announced.

As soon as she touched the ground her boots sunk into the mud. She had to work hard to lift her foot and release it from the suction trying to hold it down. Each step was a workout. Mace chuckled at her as he watched her struggle.

"Not funny," she sneered at him.

"It is kind of funny," Mace replied with a small lip twitch. "There's a small cabin up ahead. It's only about a five minute walk, although that times gonna double with the speed your going."

Tabby looked at him with a frown, then sobered as she again thought of Killian. "Do you think Killian made it out alive?"

"I'm sure of it," Mace easily assured her. "That man is one of the strongest Fallen I know. He's a warrior, and he knows how to fight. He may end up with a scratch or two, but he'll kill them all."

"You promise?" she questioned worriedly.

"No honey, I know better than to make a promise I may not be able to keep. But I could tell that man cares a great deal about you. He'll move heaven and earth to get back to you," Mace vowed.

"Okay," she conceded. Then the sound of wind chimes caught her attention. "We must be close. I hear wind chimes."

He looked at her in confusion for a minute, then threw his head back and laughed.

"What?" Tabby questioned angrily. She was really getting tired of hearing his laugh.

"That's an interesting way of putting it," Mace told her as he kept walking.

Almost ten minutes later the cabin came into view. It was small, looked like it was made out of mismatched boards, and was more of a shack than an actual cabin. There was a sketchy looking porch, but it was the item clanking together in the breeze that caught her attention.

"Are those bones?" she asked in horror.

"Honey, we're in the swamp. They're used to mark our territory and to keep the evil away," Mace explained.

Tabby followed him up the stairs, but stayed as far from the wind bones as she could. They creeped her out.

"I don't think I'm gonna like the swamp," she admitted with a small sigh of defeat.

"Which is exactly why this is the safest place there is," he chuckled. "No one wants to come here."

Tabby huffed as she stepped inside the cabin, and prayed that Killian got there soon.

Chapter 22
Killian

Killian didn't waste a minute basking in the glory of the first kill. He had the other five rogues coming at him as a unit. The knife was his only weapon, so he'd have to rely on his strength and agility to get out of this one. He was good, but even he had to admit five rogues would be a challenge.

Two came at him quickly from the front, and two came from the back, while the last one hung back. Their plan was to box him in, and he wasn't having any of that. He waited until the last minute, then he jumped. The rogues couldn't change direction mid air, so they fell in a confused heap. Of course the same could be said for him. He had nowhere to go but down when the last rouge leaped.

Killian twisted, but it wasn't enough, the rogue's claws sunk into his thigh. He grunted, but otherwise ignored the burn as he sunk his knife into the bastards neck. A quick drag with the knife and a yank with his free hand had the rogue decapitated. The body hit the ground before he did, and coated the recovering rogues in thick, sticky blood.

He hit the ground kicking out hard and caught one of them in the head. Then he was in the air again and moving to the far side of the room. This way he could fight them head on and gain more control of the situation. He landed and quickly pivoted, holding his knife out in front of him and preparing for the first attack.

It came fast. The rogue closest to him ran full out and hit him in the chest. As it clawed at his stomach he pounded on its back. His blows were powerful, and in seconds he had the rogue on the ground. He flipped him to expose his underside, then sliced into the bastards heart. A quick flick of his wrist and the heart came out on the end of the knife.

He didn't have time to do much more than throw it at the third rogue moving his way. It caught him in the face and gave Killian the chance he needed to grab the rogue around the neck and twist. The rogue barely had a chance to struggle as he snapped his neck. Using the same strategy as with the heart, he picked up the body and flung it at the last two. The momentum took the both of them down.

Not wasting a minute, Killian charged the two last rogues and dove into the middle of them. It was a vicious battle for the upper hand. Killian sliced with his knife while they sliced with their claws. He punched and tore at every piece of fur he could reach and finally got lucky. One of the wolves turned the wrong way, and he got an opening. He again aimed for the belly and sliced. Blood poured out, body parts that should never be exposed were, and the wolf collapsed.

The last wolf took advantage and clamped his sharp teeth into Killian's leg. He roared in pain and twisted, thrusting his knife into the side of the bastards head. Immediately the wolf let go and dropped at his feet. Killian stumbled twice before gaining his balance and leaning against the wall. He knew he was in bad shape, and he'd need several days of rest to recover.

He took a minute to assess his injuries. One of his legs was torn, exposing his muscle, while the other was clawed viciously and bleeding like a tap. His stomach and side were clawed as well, and he had a nasty gash on his head. His wounds weren't life threading, but they were serious.

Killian stumbled over to the bar, grabbed the few bottles of liquor that remained intact, and threw them at the bodies. Then he forced his legs to carry him to the door. At the last second he turned, raised his hands, and sent a ball of fire in the direction of the dead rogues. The liquor caught instantly and engulfed the entire place in flames.

Killian managed to get free of the building just before it exploded. The patrons were now a good distance away, and nobody noticed as he slipped down a back alley and disappeared.

Chapter 23
Killian

Killian stumbled through the alleys, sticking to the shadows. He was covered in blood and his clothes were shredded. It wouldn't do for anyone to see him. The blood loss was getting to him and he needed to find somewhere to hold up for a while. He figured Mace would take his Kitten to the swamps, but he knew there was no way he could make it that far.

He was close to the end of another alley when he noticed a group of men in front of him. He sniffed the air and deduced they were human. He went to turn back when they spotted him. Immediately they pushed off the wall and headed his way. He counted five, and they looked like they were itching for a fight.

"Hey buddy, what are you doing lurking in the fucking shadows?" one of the men yelled.

Killian was in bad shape, and although he wouldn't hesitate to take them on, there was a chance there were just too many of them. As soon as they got close they smirked at him in triumph.

"Looks like someone got to you first. It won't take much to finish you off," another laughed.

"You don't want to piss me off tonight," Killian growled in return, and knew his eyes glowed just a bit with his emotions so high.

The men paused and eyed him curiously, then they seemed to shrug what they saw off. Most humans pushed it to the back of their mind, not wanting to acknowledge he may be something else.

"Let's fuck him up," the man who had noticed him first grinned.

"Shit," Killian snarled in agitation as he pushed off the wall and prepared to defend himself.

The first man came quickly, and he threw out a punch that knocked the man back a foot. His arm screamed at the move and he hissed in pain. Not a second later the second man was on him. He kicked out and clipped the ass in the knee, dropping him to the pavement, but the rest chose that minute to jump him together. Their combined weight took him to the ground, and he heard the pavement crack beneath him.

Killian was in trouble now. The pain and blood loss were making him dizzy. He threw punches, but the humans were stronger than him at that moment, and their blows were doing a shit ton of damage to his already broken body. He covered his head and prayed this beating didn't kill him.

Black spots appeared before his eyes and he was close to just giving in, when a snarl sounded from the end of the alley. He sighed in relief when the men were ripped off him. Screams came, and Killian swore he could hear their bones snapping. As suddenly as the noise started it stopped, then a small hand reached out and touched his shoulder.

Killian dropped his arms from his head and twisted to look up. He almost expected to see Cade, but he knew the hand was way too small. He was sure his expression registered the surprise he was feeling when he looked up to see Mace's girl staring down at him in concern.

"Killian, are you okay?" she questioned in concern.

"I have no idea," he answered honestly.

"What do I need to do?" she asked as she studied him, cringing at his injuries.

"I need to hide and rest," he admitted.

She looked thoughtful for a minute before nodding. "I know a place, it's not much, but no one knows about it."

Then she grabbed him under the arms and hauled him to his feet. He swayed like a drunk man and almost went down again, but her grip prevented it.

"God, you're heavy," she complained as she adjusted his weight. She shoved her tiny body under his arm and took most of his weight. "Come on Fallen, let's get you out of here."

He went with her, dragging his feet and causing her to curse the entire way. He would have laughed at her frustrated growls if he hadn't been in so much pain. He almost felt like a human again.

Then they were stopping at an abandoned warehouse that looked like it was ready for the wrecking ball. He eyed the place with a bit of hesitation.

"Oh, don't tell me you're afraid to go in," she mocked him. He scowled at her and she laughed. "Come on tough guy, let's get you healed so you can get back to your girl."

Chapter 24
Tabby

Tabby paced the small cabin and glared at Mace. They'd been stuck there for two days now, and she was beyond frustrated. So far there was no sign of Killian, and she had no idea if he was even alive. Her thoughts ran rampant with visions of him being mauled to death by the rogues. His blood would cover the floor as his eyes slowly closed for good. She couldn't sleep because the nightmares were too vivid.

"Stop fucking pacing," Mace growled for the thousandth time today. "You're making my head spin. This cabins tiny, and you only go a couple steps before turning and heading in the other direction."

"There's nothing else to do," she complained.

"We could play poker again," he suggested on a grin as he turned on the chair he was sitting on and faced her.

"You cheat," she immediately complained.

"I don't cheat," Mace angrily responded.

"No one wins every hand," Tabby accused as she stopped her pacing and placed her hands on her hips.

"You just suck at poker," he chuckled.

"Is there no way to get in touch with Killian?" she huffed as ignored his comment. "Can't you do some angel thing and communicate telepathically or something?"

He looked at her wide eyed. "Angel thing? First off, we're Fallen honey, there's a huge difference. And second of all, angels don't communicate telepathically. Only the most powerful angels can reach us, and it's more like a summoning when we're needed."

"So there's no way to reach him?" Tabby questioned sadly.

"Unless your boy carries a cell phone, no," Mace patiently told her.

"It's been two days. Shouldn't we have heard something from him by now?" she pleaded.

"Depends on his injuries. If he was hurt badly he'd find somewhere to hunker down until he heals enough to come here. The only other reason he wouldn't come is if he's being followed and doesn't want to lead them here," Mace explained.

"Can he die?" she asked as she sat on the edge of the bed and balled her hands into fists.

Mace looked at her and sighed. "All creatures can die. Even immortals can be killed. I'm sure if you're wounded badly enough, you'd die too."

She looked at him and then dropped her shoulders in defeat. "Sometimes I wonder if this healing thing was a curse. I've been hunted since I got it, and everyone seems to want me dead."

"Well, you shouldn't look at it that way. You seem to like Killian, and I can guarantee he's going to be around for a while. It would be nice if you two didn't have to worry about the whole dying thing," Mace told her.

"I do like Killian, but he's just so intense sometimes. He's overly possessive, he's domineering, and he likes to get his own way. I also think he's extremely full of himself," she complained.

"Yep, you pretty much just described all of us immortals. But you forgot how protective we are, how much we love with all our being, and how we'll always put the ones we love before ourselves," Mace responded as he raised his brow.

She perked up at the word love and ignored the rest. "Do you love the wolf we found you with at the bar?"

Mace immediately turned serious. "I do. She's become extremely important to me, and she actually reminds me a lot of you."

"Oh, how so?" Tabby questioned curiously.

"She's beautiful, she's incredibly head strong, and she never listens," he smirked.

Tabby ignored him and asked what was on her mind the most. "Is she in trouble?"

Mace didn't hesitate to answer. "She's the alpha's daughter and she's promised to the alpha of a neighbouring pack. The packs are hoping to form a strong alliance through the marriage."

"And she doesn't want to marry him because she's in love with you," Tabby guessed.

"Exactly. And that isn't going over so well. She's been banned from seeing me," Mace growled in anger.

"Yet she came to see you the other day," she reminded him.

"She did, and I have a feeling her father will force the issue of marriage. He believes she should do her duty for the good of the pack," Mace countered.

"And you're okay with that?" Tabby questioned in surprise.

"Fuck no. That's why I told her she only had a couple days and then I was coming after her," Mace grunted.

"You'd take on two packs all by yourself?" Tabby exclaimed.

"Nope," he grinned. "Killian now owes me for getting you out of there. He can help me. They think I'm human, so it will be a huge surprise when we walk in there and show them what we are."

Jesus, she thought. Mace was supposed to help, not cause more problems. Things were getting damn crazy, and she still didn't know about the prophecy because Mace refused to tell her until Killian was back. She was ready to say screw it and go looking for him herself.

Chapter 25
Killian

Killian groaned as he tried to roll on his side. He'd been laying on a cot in this rundown warehouse for two days now, and he was fucking sick of it. Mace would keep Tabby safe, he was sure of it, but it was time to get back to them. He growled at Kathleen as she walked through the door. The little wolf had got him some place safe, and she had taken the time to clean and tend to his wounds, but he was frustrated with her.

"Don't you growl at me," Kathleen admonished. "I'll just growl right back. Besides, I brought you food," she grinned as she tossed a paper bag in his direction.

Killian reached up and snatched it before it hit him in the face. "You remind me a lot of my Kitten," he told her.

She turned and smirked at him as she rifled through her own paper bag. "Well, she must really be something special."

He couldn't help grinning at the girl. She had as much spunk and attitude as his girl did. Mace did well in choosing her.

"You and Mace must be really close," Killian pushed as he took a bite of the burger he had opened. Immediately her face closed down and she lost the smile.

"We are, but it's complicated," Kathleen told him as she turned away and opened her own burger.

"I've got time," he grinned.

She looked at him then shrugged. "I'm promised to the alpha of another pack. I was willing to mate him for the sake of our packs," she explained.

"Then you met Mace," Killian concluded.

She threw up her arms in agitation. "He caught me fighting off three rogues and he stepped in. He looked after my wounds and we got close. He's hard not to like."

"So now you want him instead of the alpha," Killian pried gently.

"I do, but it may not be possible. My father isn't willing to listen and the alpha refuses to back down," Kathleen sighed.

"Do they know Mace is a Fallen?" Killian questioned.

"No," Kathleen denied. "I don't think that will go over well. We're not supposed to mate out of our race. A human's bad enough, but to tell them he's a Fallen?" Kathleen shook her head sadly. "They'd never accept him."

"You can't just leave?" Killian pushed. It's what he would do.

"I'd be considered rogue, and then I'd be hunted," she told him.

"I have a friend," he admitted. "His name's Cade. He's an alpha and enforcer. He may be able to help."

She frowned at him as she dropped her burger. "Enforcers aren't real," she declared.

"Right," Killian smirked. "Neither are Fallen and werewolves. I guarantee he's real, and so are his pack mates, who just happen to be enforcers too."

"You think he'd help," she questioned with a tiny bit of hope to her voice.

"He believes in love, I think he'd be happy to help," he honestly told her. "But I can't ask him while I'm hiding out in this god awful warehouse healing."

She laughed at him then. "Sneaky. You're good at manipulation."

"Don't tell me Mace wouldn't be happy to see you got out of that bar safely," Killian added with a raised brow.

Once more her smile dropped, and it was starting to piss him off. "I'll make sure you get out of the here safely. Then I have to get back to my pack. I've still got some things I can do to try to stop this. I need to do everything I can without involving Mace first."

"I don't think Mace would agree," Killian told her. "That man definitely isn't someone to sit back and wait patiently."

Kathleen smiled again. "True, which is why I'm doing this now. He's distracted, and it gives me time to take a stand without him. I need to do this my way first," she pushed once more.

"Okay," Killian replied, not agreeing with her at all. "Then lets finish eating. I'm leaving today and going after my girl."

"Are you strong enough?" she asked cautiously.

"I'll fucking have to be," he grunted. "If you're that concerned you can come with me just in case I need help."

She tilted her head. "Pushy," she declared as she picked her burger back up and took another bite.

"You have no idea," Killian growled. He had questioned her about the prophecy, but she didn't know anything about it, and he wasn't surprised. It made him more determined to get to Mace. And when he did, he was finding out what the hell it was and what it had to do with him.

Chapter 26
Tabby

Tabby waited until Mace was asleep before attempting her escape. She didn't want to admit she was worried about Killian, but she was. The man was a Fallen, so she figured that unless he was dead he should have found them by now. Besides that, she couldn't wait around anymore. The hut was creepy, and the noises she heard from the swamp were freaking her out.

She moved across the floor and stopped at the door. It was wide open, but the screen was latched shut. At first, it had terrified her that something or someone would come through the flimsy screen, but after two days, nothing did. Maybe the bone wind chimes actually worked. They certainly scared her enough.

Tabby lifted the hook and unlatched the door, then slowly opened it. Immediately the damn thing screeched, and she froze as Mace rolled over in his sleep. He was close to the door and sleeping on the floor, and she had to step over him to reach it. She figured he was a light sleeper, but he continued his soft snore and she breathed a sigh of relief. Throwing caution to the wind she yanked the screen, opening it as quickly as she could. Surprisingly, the faster she went the less sound it made. She grinned as she stepped out on the porch and grabbed a large rock. She'd watched Mace place it front of the door as a door stop a couple times, so that's what she did too. She didn't want to risk the noise if she tried to close it again.

A few seconds later she was down the steps and headed into the trees. The moon was full and it illuminated the sky enough that she could see fairly easily. She gingerly stepped into the mucky moss as she swatted at the mosquitos that swarmed around her head. If she ever got out of this place, she hoped to never see it again. A snap came from somewhere to her left, and she jumped high into the air. A shrill cry followed it, and then there was a thrashing in the shallow water. She figured a lucky alligator just found its dinner, and she was just glad it wasn't her.

Tabby had walked about ten minutes when she heard a rustling high above her. Stopping, she held as still as she could as she tried to peer up into the trees. It was almost impossible to pick out anything distinguishable, except for the leaves. The breeze blew gently, and with the trees swaying, she just couldn't see anything. Panicking now, she turned and was about to head back when the angel she'd seen before dropped down in front of her.

She shrieked at his sudden appearance, then took a couple steps back. He frowned as he watched her move, then he took a step towards her. She did the only thing she could think of. She pulled out her squirt gun, firing it at him. The water caught him in the chin, and he had the gall to chuckle at her.

"I'm an angel sweetheart. Holy water won't harm me," he patiently told her. Then he took another step towards her as he dropped his smile. "You were supposed to die. Why can't you just give up and let me do my job?"

"Because I'm not ready to die," Tabby challenged as she slid her blade from the strap on her hip. "I've still got a bucket list I need to complete."

He tilted his head and studied her. "Are you serious?" he asked curiously.

"Yep, and killing an angel's the first thing on it," she taunted him.

Tabby lunged suddenly, but before she even came close strong arms wrapped around her waist and she was lifted from the ground.

"You got her?" she heard Mace growl from somewhere close by.

"Yes, I fucking got her," Killian growled back as his arms tightened.

Tabby immediately sagged in relief, more than happy to be in his arms. "You're okay," she whispered as she tried to twist so she could see him.

"I'm okay," he responded. "But I'm going to fucking tan your ass for leaving the cabin."

"The hut from hell," she countered as she shot a glare his way. "And you aren't getting anywhere near my ass."

Tabby could feel his chest vibrate, and she hated that he was laughing at her. "Can we get away from the angel that wants me dead?" she questioned angrily.

Tabby didn't get to say anymore, because suddenly she was thrown into the air. She cried out as Mace leaped up and caught her, then he was spinning and landing in the opposite direction. She closed her eyes and held on as he increased his speed and moved at a dizzying pace. She'd been through this before with him, so this time she was able to punch him in the arm while calling him every nasty name she could come up with.

Chapter 27
Killian

Killian watched as Mace disappeared into the forest with his Kitten held tightly in his arms. It burned him to see another man touching her, but it was a necessity. Once they were out of sight he turned to face one of the few men he had once called a friend.

"Stop trying to kill my mate," he growled at Azriel.

"I'm doing my job. A job you seem to have trouble completing," Azriel shot back.

"Because she's my mate," Killian countered with a glare.

"Well, she wasn't yours when you first saw her. You should have done it then. We could have avoided all this," Azriel countered as he threw up his arms in frustration.

"Do you know anything about mates?" Killian furiously questioned him.

"Of course not," Azriel immediately replied. "We aren't meant to have mates."

"Everyone's meant to have a mate," Killian grunted in return. "From the first moment I laid eyes on her there was something about her that called to me. I recognized immediately that I couldn't kill her. I just hadn't had feelings in so long I didn't understand what it was."

"That's ridiculous," Azriel huffed as he paced, ignoring the mosquitoes flying around his head.

"That's because you haven't experienced it. I want a front row seat when this happens to you," Killian chuckled, but Azriel just turned and scowled at him.

"I have a job to do, and I'm not one to let a mate impede that," he denied.

"Right," Killian chuckled. "You're going to be in even more trouble than I am." Then he rubbed his chin and thought for a moment. "You're repulsed by vampires. Maybe she'll be a vampire. Or you think witches are heretics. I bet she's a witch."

"Stop that," Azriel finally yelled, and Killian knew he was getting to him. He dropped his grin and turned serious.

"Stay away from my mate," he repeated. "You've always been a good friend, but if I have to choose, I will choose her. You go after her again and I'll tear you to pieces."

"You'd honestly put a human's life over mine," Azriel snarled in surprise as he stopped his pacing and faced him.

"In a heartbeat," Killian promised. "What do you know of the prophecy?" he suddenly questioned, figuring the angel had to know something.

"I don't know about any prophecy," Azriel denied as he turned away. But Killian had seen the angel's mouth harden and he knew he was lying. Instantly he called him out on it.

"You're lying," Killian accused him.

"And you're a fool," Azriel growled. "Kill the girl and all of this will be over."

Killian studied his old friend for a few minutes. "Everyone seems to be after her, either to see her dead or to find the key to immortality. Why is that?"

"She's not immortal. She just heals quickly," Azriel corrected. "She can be killed if the wound is serious enough."

"But how did word spread so quickly? Immortals are coming out of every corner to get a piece of her," Killian asked, a bad feeling settling in his stomach.

"Every angel has a job to do. You were one of the best and you disobeyed a direct order. Now angel's are starting to questions themselves and it's causing turmoil. The girl needs to die, and it needs to happen now," Azriel sneered.

"So you got word to every group of immortals you could," Killian accused. "It was you that sent everybody after her."

"I did what I had to do," Azriel snarled back. "In time, I hope you realize that."

Killian moved fast, leaping in the angel's direction, but he was too late. Azriel had expected the move and had already spread his wings and shot high in the sky. Killian missed his foot by about an inch before he fell back to the ground. He landed on his knee in the mud, and the heavy thud he made caused birds to fly from the trees, and alligators to splash back into the water. He ignored them all, furious about what he had just discovered.

Azriel had been his closest friend, and he felt the betrayal in his gut. Even when he was cast out, he knew Azriel had only done so because of the rules. But to put a kill out on his mate was unacceptable. He lifted his head and glared at the sky.

"Run far brother, because I'm coming for you. And I'm going to show you what hell feels like," he roared.

Chapter 28
Tabby

Tabby was back to pacing the hut from hell and throwing things at Mace. He easily ducked each time, but it made her feel better. The cup she just threw bounced off the door and dropped harmlessly to the floor. She snarled and then turned to head back in the opposite direction.

"Why is the cabin so small?" she complained. "It's hard to pace when you're at the other side in five steps."

Mace grinned at her. "Then sit the fuck down and stop that shit. We've had this argument before."

She glared at him and looked around to throw something else.

"Woman, everything that was in your reach is now laying on the floor all around me. Give it the fuck up and plant your ass in a chair," Mace ordered.

Tabby placed her hands on her hips, glared, and was about to say something when the door was shoved open and Killian prowled inside. He glanced at Mace, nodded, then headed straight to her. She tried to back up, nervous about the intense way he was looking at her, but he moved too fast. One minute she was standing there, the next she was up in his arms and his lips were slammed against hers. She didn't even stop to think, she just held on and kissed him back. His fist tangled in her hair, his other hand was around her back, and his mouth devoured hers. She was completely lost to the overwhelming feelings he was igniting in her.

"For fuck's sake, you aren't alone," Mace growled, and that effectively ended their kiss.

Killian pulled back, dropped her to her feet, and stared down at her. "We'll continue that later."

"Um, okay," was all she got out, before the ass smirked at her.

"Tell me about the prophecy," Killian demanded, as he swung his gaze to his friend and she lost his eyes. She dropped into the closest chair and looked at the other Fallen as well.

"I've only glimpsed it, but I've heard the higher ups discussing it. An angel will find his soulmate and together they will produce a child that will be more powerful than any other immortal. The child will band the immortals together and change the world," Mace explained.

Killian frowned, then asked the question he had been thinking. "So what's that got to do with me?"

Mace sighed then explained more. "The angel that sires the boy is said to be a Trojan Soldier. It reveals that he would fall because he saved a girl that awakened his feelings. It's the beginning of the prophecy. The rest explains that he will find his soul mate and sire the child."

"Well, I am the only Trojan Soldier who became an angel," Killian proudly stated. "And I definitely fell because my Kitten awakened my feelings."

"I agree," Mace nodded. "The prophecy points at you without actually using your name."

"So why did Azriel order a kill on Tabby?" Killian growled. "It's obvious from both my feeling and the prophecy that she's my soulmate."

"No I'm not," Tabby told them sadly. "I'm not an angel. Azriel wants me dead so I'm out of the way, and you're free to find the angel you're meant to be with."

"That makes sense," Mace agreed.

"I started the prophecy," Tabby added. "But I'm not a part of it. Azriel wants the prophecy to play out. He's helping you by killing me."

Killian suddenly roared. Then he picked up a chair and threw it through the window. Tabby jumped to her feet and stared at him in shock. He was angry, and not an angry like she'd ever seen before. He looked like he was about to explode, and that scared the hell out of her.

"You're my fucking soul mate, and I don't give a shit about the prophecy. It's a fucking piece of paper that some asshole wrote some random words on. It's garbage, and not something I'm going to waste my time thinking about," he snarled.

Tabby took a tentative step towards him, and when he didn't move she closed the distance. Slowly she raised her hand and placed it on his heart. "I've been fighting my feelings for you, but I feel it too. Somehow I know I'm meant to be with you. We'll figure this out, but we'll do it together. And if something happens to me, we'll know that it wasn't meant to be."

Killian stared at her for only a minute before yanking her hard against his chest and wrapping his massive arms around her once more. "It's meant to be," he insisted.

"We'll find out one way or another," she whispered as a lone tear slid down her cheek. She didn't mean for him to hear, but he huffed and rested his chin against her head. If she only had a short time left with him, she vowed to make the most of it.

Chapter 29
Killian

"If you two are fine here for a while, I need to go check on my little wolf," Mace declared with a frown. "I have to make sure she didn't get hurt at the bar."

"Kathleen's fine," Killian assured her. "She found me in an alley and took me to a safe location. She stayed with me while I was there and was a godsend. I would have been in serious trouble if she hadn't showed up."

"Jesus," Mace growled. "She's in the thick of everything."

"She is, but she's strong and fearsome. Kathleen will make a good mate and partner," Killian assured him. "Just like my Kitten will for me."

He glanced at Tabby and saw the sad look hadn't left her eyes. Damn the fucking prophecy and its lies. It was just a piece of paper someone had decorated with ink, it meant nothing. He moved across the room in a blur and wrapped his arms around her.

"You've accepted me now, I'm keeping you," he breathed in her ear. "Nothing will break our bond, not even a stupid prophecy."

She didn't say a word, but she hugged him back and placed her head on his chest, right over his heart. His strong girl needed his assurance.

"My little wolf didn't come with you," Mace stated, interrupting their moment. "Where did she go?"

"She was headed back to the pack to talk to her father. She's determined to change his mind," Killian explained.

Mace frowned. "If he hasn't yet, he's not going to. She's wasting her breath."

"I agree, but I couldn't stop her. I have my own problems right now to deal with," Killian replied.

"Understood," Mace agreed. "But if I need to go after her, you're coming with me. You owe me," he ordered.

Killian nodded. "You have my promise, but I need to find someplace safe to hide Tabby first."

"I don't need babysitting," his Kitten roared as she moved back and punched him in the arm. "I'll go with you."

"Oh no you won't," he replied. "You've got a death order on your head. The last thing you need to do is walk into a pack of wolves and present yourself to them."

"I've got the spells and amulets Celeste gave me. I'll carry a gun armed with silver bullets, and I can disguise myself if I need to. No one will know it's me," Tabby declared.

"They'll smell you," Mace informed her. "They won't even need to see you."

"And the spells and amulets will take care of that," she reinforced. "Celeste is good at what she does. They won't realize it's me."

"I'm not taking a fucking chance with your life Kitten," Killian growled.

"Well then get more friends to go with you," Tabby growled back. "You must know others who will stand at your back."

Killian glared at her. "I know some wolves who will stand with me, they've had my back before. If it doesn't take them away from their families for too long, I'm sure they'll agree to come."

"Well make the calls," Mace ordered as he pulled a cell from his pocket and tossed it to him. "Let's do this now before things get too messy or she's mated to the alpha. If that happens, I'll rip him limb from limb and probably break my little wolf's heart. Once they're mated it's hard to undo."

"It's a life bond," Tabby agreed. "And she's in love with you. I think being forced to mate another would break her, not his death. If the mating wasn't meant to be it will hold, but it will be the bite that ties them, not the bond." When they looked at her in surprise, she shrugged her shoulders. "I've done a lot of reading."

"That's not true," Killian denied, drawing both their attention. "Actually, the wolf I'm calling had his mate taken before they were mated. The rogue that took her tried to mate her by giving her the bite. It didn't take and healed right away. There's a good chance the same could happen if this alpha tries to mark Kathleen."

"Doesn't matter," Mace growled as he paced the floor. "I'm not giving him the chance to bite her. Make the call Killian," he ordered.

Killian nodded and hit some buttons on the phone. It took only a minute for the call to go through and Cade to answer.

"I don't know who this is, but this better be good," Cade growled into the other end.

"It's Killian. I thought you'd want to know a female wolf is being forced to mate an alpha." Before Cade could answer, Killian kept going. "Her mate is a Fallen, and he's standing beside me. You interested in helping us stop it."

"Goddamned wolves," Cade roared. "They don't give a shit about true mates. A Fallen and a wolf mating is something I've never heard of, but you can count me in. Tell me where you are and I'll bring James and Paul with me."

"Appreciated," Killian replied. He relayed their location and waited a minute.

"We'll be there in about twelve hours. You still got the girl with you?" Cade inquired.

"I do," Killian agreed.

"Then this should be fun," Cade chuckled.

Killian let out a string of curse words, but Cade had already hung up on him.

Chapter 30
Tabby

The guys slept while they waited for the other three wolves to arrive. Killian was still recovering, but he looked good. Whatever wounds he suffered had healed, and the only evidence of the fight was his slower movements. He assured her the sleep would help with that, and he'd be as good as new when he woke up. Mace was asleep too, but she figured he did that just so he wouldn't have to deal with her anymore.

Tabby tried curling up on the tiny bed next to Killian, and no matter how comfortable she was wrapped up in his huge arms, she couldn't get any sleep. She was too on edge and too wired. She paced for a while, and then she sat on the porch for a while. That didn't last long, as the bugs were vicious and had attacked the minute she sat down. Also, the frigging bones creeped her out. They blew in the wind and the noise sent shivers up her spine. At least when she was inside she could pretend they were wind chimes, outside she had a clear view, and she didn't like it.

When the men finally woke up, she was ready to pull her hair out. The second Killian moved she was leaning over the bed and anxiously staring into his face. When he opened his eyes and saw her so close, he jerked away and slammed his head into the wall.

"What the fuck are you doing Kitten?" he complained as he rubbed the back of his head.

She frowned at him. "I'm bored out of my mind. You both fell asleep and there's absolutely nothing to do in this hut from hell."

"And you couldn't give me a minute until I was wake before shoving your face in mine. You about gave me a heart attack," Killian growled.

"I got excited," Tabby pouted as she stepped back and gave him some room.

"Shut up over there," Mace complained from his curled up position on the floor. "I'm trying to sleep."

"You've been asleep for about ten hours," Tabby snickered. "It's time to get up and go meet the wolves."

That got him moving. "I'm up," Mace replied as he pushed off the floor and stood to his full height. "Let's go get my girl."

"Sure, you're all gung-ho when it's your girl. You wouldn't step foot outside when it was me," Tabby sneered.

"That's because one foot out that door and trouble would be there waiting. You're a walking death trap," Mace snickered. "I've never even met a snake man before, but you got attacked by one. Walking death trap," he repeated.

"You weren't even around when that happened," she argued, but Mace was conveniently ignoring her now.

Killian chuckled. "If we're heading out you need to get every protective amulet, spell, and weapon you have and load up," he advised her.

"I've had ten hours to myself. What do you think I've been doing this whole time?" she complained as she opened the top buttons on her shirt and showed off her chest.

"Jesus," Killian laughed. "That should about do it."

Tabby had about ten necklaces on, each containing a satchel of items. Four amulets on. And she had a shit ton of sigils written on her skin. She wasn't taking any chances.

"Doesn't your neck hurt wearing all that shit?" Mace questioned.

"A little," she admitted. "But I'm not ready to die."

That sobered the Fallen up, and he frowned at her. Unlike him though, Killian charged across the room and pulled her up against his chest. His arms wrapped around he, and his hand fisted in her hair.

"You're not dying," Killian growled. "I didn't save you to watch you die."

"You may not have a say about that," Tabby whispered. "My time was up, you're just prolonging it."

"Fuck that," he growled. "You belong with me Kitten, and I intend to fight off every ass that comes for you."

"I don't want you hurt," she whispered into his tee.

"I'm hard to kill," he snickered. "And I've been around for a long time. I've learned some tricks over the years. I can hold my own."

"Can we fucking leave," Mace complained as he stood by the door impatiently tapping is foot. "I want to get to Kathleen before the alpha does anything stupid."

"Like try to mate her?" Tabby helpfully asked.

"Exactly," Mace growled back. Then he opened the door and was gone.

"Want a piggy back through the muck," Killian asked as he bent down and grinned at her.

"Does a bear shit in the woods?" she replied as she stepped back, took a running leap, and jumped on him. The ass didn't even grunt. When she settled he twisted around to look at her, and the look he gave her caused goosebumps to pepper her skin.

"I won't let them hurt you," Killian swore.

"I know," Tabby immediately assured him as she rested her head on his shoulder. "But things don't always work out the way we want them to."

His chest rumbled with his growl and she knew he didn't agree, but she was thankful when he said no more and headed for the door. A minute later the three of them headed down the path and were on their way to meet the wolves. Mace was tense, and she felt for the Fallen. She just hoped they arrived in time.

Chapter 31
Killian

An hour into their trek they ran into the wolves. The journey had been an easy one, and they didn't move too fast, having lots of time to spare. The enforcers were silent on their feet, and neither Fallen heard their approach. When they jumped out of the woods and surrounded them Tabby screamed blue murder and fell off his back. He scowled at Shane, who had been closest to her.

"Did you need to bring him?" Killian growled at Cade. "I thought it would only be the three of you."

"That was the plan," Cade chuckled. "But you know Shane whines when we leave him out."

Killian reached down and hauled his Kitten to her feet. Then he turned her around and brushed off her ass for good measure. She scowled up at him and knocked his hands away.

"You all suck," she complained.

James held up his arms in surrender. "It was all his idea," he defended as he pointed an accusing finger at Shane.

"Well, you didn't have to agree," Tabby pouted.

Killian shook his head as he pulled his girl close. "I'd like you to meet Tabby. And I don't think you've met Mace. It's his little wolf we're going after."

The wolves all stepped forward and exchanged greetings with Mace, but made sure they were at a distance as they greeted Tabby. They were respectful of Killian's short temper when it came to his mate, and he appreciated that.

"I thought we were to meet you at the cabin?" Paul questioned.

"Mace wasn't in the mood to wait," Killian acknowledged. "You'd be the same if it was one of your mates."

"Damn straight," Cade agreed. "What's the plan?"

"I announce Kathleen is my true mate. If they don't accept that, I let them see what I am, and then I tear them all to shreds," Mace growled.

"I like his plan," Shane announced. "Sounds like things are going to get messy."

"They don't know you're a Fallen?" James asked with a raised brow.

"They haven't met me. It was decided early in our relationship that Kathleen would go to the alpha herself. And she hid it from me for a while. The little minx thought she could dissuade her father from falling through all on her own," Mace sighed.

"And that didn't go so well," James acknowledged.

"No," Mace sneered. "She hasn't returned, and I'm not getting happy thoughts. We need to get to her before the alpha bites her."

"And what about our new little immortal?" Cade questioned. "You're walking her right into a den of wolves."

"I am," Killian agreed. "But the safest place for her is with me. I'm not leaving her unprotected. Azriel put a goddamned kill order out on her."

"Fuck," Cade swore. "I was under the impression you and he were close. He explain why?"

"Only that her time was up. The job wasn't completed, and he wants it done," Killian explained.

"There must be more to it," Shane decided. "Even if he's the head honcho up there, your friendship should come first."

"Unless there's more he's not saying," Killian huffed.

"It's the prophecy," Tabby said, jumping into the conversation. "He wants me out of the way so you can find your real mate and everything can fall into line. I'm a complication."

Killian roared and Tabby took a tentative step away from him, pissing him off even more. "You're my mate and the ass needs to realize that. He broke our friendship the minute he went after you. I'm not fucking losing you."

"We'll protect her like our own," Cade vowed. "I think it's a smart move taking her with us. And if Azriel decides to makes an appearance, he'll have all of us to go through." The other wolves nodded in agreement, and Killian nodded back.

"Now lets go get your mate back," James told Mace. "After that we can put our heads together and see if we can figure out a way to help you and your girl."

"Appreciated," Killian replied.

"I'll owe you," Mace growled. "This is asking a lot."

"It's actually not," Paul countered. "We enforce the laws of the packs. Forcing someone to mate is something we don't abide by. And if she explained she had a mate, it's worse. They know what they're doing is wrong, and they're still going through with it. It's our duty to step in."

Mace grinned. "Well, lets get going then," he demanded as he stormed off toward the packs.

Shane grinned and went after him, and the rest followed. Things were about to get interesting, and Killian hoped like hell they could keep Tabby safe, because if she died, he'd die too. But he'd take a hell of a lot of wolves with him.

Chapter 32
Tabby

It didn't take the group long to reach the main pack lands. Halfway through the journey the Enforcers stripped down and shifted, and Mace carried a backpack containing their clothes. Killian insisted on carrying Tabby, and she had to admit she didn't hate the idea. She'd always seemed to be with Mace when they did the dizzying speed run, so it was nice to curl into Killian.

"You comfy," Killian chuckled as he smirked down at her. Tabby had her eyes closed, but she knew the smirk was there.

"Comfy enough," she answered as she poked him in the chest. "Although your chest is a little hard. It's difficult to curl into a rock."

Killian lost his smile as he narrowed his eyes and glared at her while the rest of the men chuckled. Immediately she opened hers, surprised the men had shifted back.

"Are we here?" Tabby questioned as he dumped her to her feet.

"We're at Kathleen's father pack, and I'm surprised no one's stopped us yet. They've followed us for the last fifteen minutes," Mace announced.

"Then they would have seen you move faster," she acknowledged with some concern as she stared up at Killian.

Shane chuckled then. "You've had your eyes closed for the whole journey. We shifted a while ago, and both the Fallen slowed."

"So I could have walked," she accused Killian.

"No," Killian growled. "We're in wolf territory now, and I wanted you close. I'm not taking any chances with your life."

"I'm going to be okay," Tabby whispered as she moved into his arms once more.

"We've got company," Cade growled as a dozen wolves stepped out of the surrounding trees.

The Enforcers stood their ground and watched as the wolves closed in on them. Then a tall, extremely muscled man stepped into the middle of things.

"I'm Nico, the alpha's second," he explained. "You're trespassing on pack lands and I want to know why."

Mace glared at the man as he took a step in his direction, but Cade placed his hand on Mace's shoulder, stopping him. The look he gave Mace was one of warning.

"Mace is Kathleen's true mate, and he's come to get her," Cade told the wolf.

Nico eyed Mace with distain, then turned his attention back to Cade. "Human, and he brought wolves to back him up." Then he seemed to notice Tabby hiding behind Killian. "You want to trade?"

When Killian stepped forward, his whole body was tense. Tabby locked her arms around his waist and held on, hoping she could hold him back.

"Not the right thing to say big guy," she yelled at Nico warningly.

"Take us to the alpha," James ordered, in an attempt to get Nico's attention off her.

"You don't make demands," Nico growled. "We have you out numbered and surrounded."

"Oh really," Shane smirked as he looked around. "I'll take the first five, then I'll help you guys out when I'm done."

Cade smirked. "You always take the first five. Then you're huffing like an old man and too tired to help us."

Shane placed his hands on his waist and cocked his hip, and Tabby almost lost it, it was so funny.

"I'm laughing not huffing," Shane threw back. "I always dispatch my five before you even take out three."

"Jesus," Nico interrupted, then he turned to one of the wolves. "Get the alpha and bring him here."

While they waited, Killian shifted Tabby, and the Enforcers and Mace moved so they surrounded her. It was more than obvious they were protecting her, and Nico narrowed his eyes at them.

"We won't hurt her unless she's a threat," Nico sneered. "We don't hurt women."

"Yet you gave my mate to someone else," Mace thundered. "How is that not hurting women?"

"The alpha decided to offer his daughter to tie the two packs together. The mating will bring a strong alliance," Nico stated. "Kathleen will be better off mated to a wolf than a human. You can't protect her."

"I can protect her better than all of you put together," Mace threatened as his eyes turned black.

"What the hell is going on?" the alpha thundered as he joined them. His eyes were blazing, and he was staring right into Mace's black ones.

"You gave my mate to another," Mace sneered. "I'm here to get her back."

"My daughter has a duty to this pack. No human will interfere with that," the alpha declared.

Mace turned to Tabby, and the look in his eyes was pure fury. "You're the only human here. You going to interfere."

"Yep," she nodded as she grinned at him and pulled away from Killian. "And I've brought a silver dagger, and a gun loaded with silver bullets." She pulled the items out and held them up proudly. "This human came prepared. Who do you want me to kill first?"

Mace smirked, but the alpha clearly looked ready to blow.

Chapter 33
Killian

Killian was furious with Mace for putting his girl in the spotlight. Now all the wolves were focused on her, and that didn't sit well with him. His eyes turned as black as Mace's, and he was ready to take them all on himself.

"Great," Shane muttered. "Now you've angered them both. You know this one isn't going to let his girl fight," he huffed as he pointed at Killian.

"What do you have to do with this anyway?" the alpha demanded of Shane.

Cade stepped up then, and his body seemed to grow in size as he glared at the alpha. "Did you know your daughter already found her mate?"

"She told me," the alpha acknowledged. "But she stated he wasn't a wolf, so that bit of information didn't mean a damn thing."

"He's her true mate, and you're rejected the mating," Cade accused. "Have I got that right?"

"I did," the alpha growled as he took a threatening pose. "My daughter needs to put the pack first."

"My mate's human," James admitted, joining the argument. "I'm stronger with her by my side. She protects me just as much as I protect her. Is it only because you think her mate's human that you reject him?"

"That's twice you've implied he isn't human, and yet I sense nothing else," the alpha insisted.

"It doesn't matter what he is," Cade interjected. "The point is you broke pack laws when you ignored the true mate bond. You knew she had a mate, and you still forced a different mating. Every wolf here backed you up."

The alpha tilted his head then and glared at Cade curiously. "You need to damn well explain who you are."

Cade smiled back and then turned to the other Enforcers. "We represent the council and we enforce pack laws. We have full power to act if needed and to punish those that ignore those laws."

"Enforcers," the alpha sputtered in disbelief. "How the hell did you find out about this?"

"Kathleen's true mate is a good friend of ours. We all decided to tag along and offer our support. You should consider that a good thing too. He would have come here himself, and that wouldn't have been a good idea," Cade snickered.

"Why? Because once we killed him you'd have to retaliate," Nico growled.

"No, because he'd kill you all and we'd have to clean up the mess," James grinned.

"Enough," Mace roared. "Tell me where my mate is and then stay the hell out of my way. And you better pray the bite hasn't already happened."

"She's about twenty minutes north east of here," Nico explained. "And because of the mating, the alpha will have his most trusted wolves guarding his main house. It will take an army to get past them."

Mace raised his hands and huge black clouds rolled across the sky. The sun disappeared and the wind picked up. Then with a flick of his wrist, a huge bolt of lightning shot from the sky and hit the ground in the direction Nico had pointed out.

"Kathleen will know I'm coming now," Mace told them. "She's aware of what I can do."

"I'm going with you," Killian announced. "Do you need to stay and met out any punishment?" he asked Cade. "Or are you joining us?"

"I'll call the council and let them know what's going on. They can decide the alpha and his packs fate," Cade growled.

"Right," Killian agreed. "Lead the way Mace, we're all with you."

Mace nodded, then turned in the direction of his girl and instantly became a blur.

"Up you go Kitten," Killian ordered, as he scooped up his own girl, and swung her around to his back. "Close your eyes, and don't get down, I can fight with you right where you are."

She nodded and didn't argue, which made Killian relax slightly. He bent and she climbed on, curing her body around him. She wrapped her legs around his waist and hooked her arms around his chest.

"We'll see you there," he shouted at Cade and the others, then he too disappeared into the trees.

"Fallen," he heard whispered by the alpha in disbelief, and Killian grinned. Their abilities had given them away, and he couldn't care less. It was always a shock to those that discovered what they were.

Chapter 34
Killian

Killian and Mace slowed as soon as they reached pack lands. He made sure his Kitten stayed on his back, and she didn't once complain. It was a relief, and he was grateful she was listening. He didn't need to worry about her as well. Mace needed him and he'd do all he could to help. Killian could hear The Enforcers approaching, but he couldn't see them yet.

"We going in, or are we waiting for them?" Killian questioned Mace. He preferred to wait for the wolves, but he understood waiting could cost Kathleen.

"I'm not waiting," Mace replied. "You'd charge in there if it was Tabby."

"I would," Killian agreed. He received a squeeze from his girl for his comment. "Lead the way."

The two proceeded cautiously and made their way slowly through the village. Every house they passed was dark, and not one wolf stopped them. It was eerily quiet, and that didn't sit well with either fallen.

"The alpha should be in a house just around the corner," Mace explained as he stopped. "You get the feeling that's where all the wolves are?"

"I think we're walking right towards a goddamned army," Killian sneered. "I bet the entire pack's guarding the house."

Mace nodded and motioned towards Tabby. "I think maybe we should hide her. This won't be an easy fight, and there's a good chance she could get hurt."

Killian frowned and found himself at a loss. He agreed with Mace, but he also felt she was safer with him. All it would take was one wolf to get behind him, and she'd be in trouble.

"I've got a gun and I'm a good shot," Tabby whispered, surprising him. "But you need to make the decision. I can hole up somewhere and shoot whoever gets close. Or I can stay on your back and do it. Which would be better for you?"

Mace grinned at her, and Killian knew he would answer instead. "Stay on his back. It will ease his mind. And you can take out wolves too. The more we take down the better."

"We'll stay behind you," Cade added as he stepped up with the rest of the Enforcers. "No one will get close to her. We fight together and as soon as there's a break, the two of you get into that house."

"The bulk of them should be outside. There shouldn't be many in the house," James added. "If you need to kill the alpha, you do it. The pack will stop attacking the minute that happens."

Mace nodded. "Enough talking. Let's do this," he ordered, and Killian saw the tension in his body. The Fallen was locked tight and he was terrified for his mate.

As soon as they stepped around the corner at least forty wolves lifted their heads. They were all shifted, and they were surrounding the large pack house. Mace growled and they all growled back. Then he raised his hands and shot a bolt of lightening right into the middle of them. It hit one wolf in the back and he dropped dead, smoke rising from a hole.

"Move," Killian ordered the Enforcers as the pack headed for them at a dead run. Killian and Mace both raised their hands and shot a blast at the group. It hit the group and knocked several wolves back, but the rest kept coming.

"We're shifting," Paul yelled as the four Enforcers leaped. "Don't kill us by accident."

Then the battle was on. The group met and blood flew in all directions. Killian stopped pushing out and instead shot a ball of fire at the nearest wolf. When a wolf leaped at him, he caught it by the throat and slammed it down on the ground.

The movement shifted his Kitten, and he didn't like that. She'd need both hands to hold on, and wouldn't be able to help. Then a tiny hand wrapped around his neck and grabbed the edge of his tee, balling it into her fist. He smirked as she brought up her free hand and shot at a wolf about to pounce. She hit him right in the head, and he dropped dead.

"Don't stop," Tabby yelled in his ear as she fired at another one. "Blast them, shoot fire, decimate some more."

His girl was a warrior, and he couldn't be happier. He raised his arms once more and concentrated on a wolf moving towards Mace. His blast lifted the wolf off the ground and it howled in panic. Killian flung his hands to the side and the wolf flew a couple feet, slamming into another wolf. Both fell and his girl whooped in glee.

Killian glanced back to see the Enforcers holding their own. Paul had a gash on his side and Shane was bleeding from one leg, but there were dead wolves all around them. It was time to head for the house, and he hoped like hell Kathleen was unharmed.

Chapter 35
Tabby

Tabby clung to Killian's back as he raced up the front steps of the house behind Mace. The two were a force to be reckoned with as they threw the last few wolves aside and kicked in the front door. She glanced behind them, but the Enforcers were stopping the last of the pack from following them.

"Kathleen," Mace roared as he stopped in the massive entryway and tilted his head. Killian's was at the same angle, so she figured they were listening to see which direction to head.

She heard nothing except the last of the battle outside, but suddenly they were on the move again and charging up the stairs. They hit the landing and Mace jumped, landing easily on the top floor. She lost sight of him for a minute as Killian continued to run up the rest of the stairs.

When they reached the top she could hear the distinctive sounds of a fight. Glass broke, there were thuds, and curse words were thrown around like water. The door at the end of the hall was open and Mace was standing there like a raging bull, glaring into the room.

It took Killian only a second to move down the hall and reach his friend's side. When he did he released her, and she gratefully dropped to her feet. She pushed between the two Fallen and stared at the scene in front of her.

Tabby cringed at the sight of Kathleen and the alpha. Both were covered in blood and both were locked in a deadly battle. They were in their human forms, and it appeared the alpha was gaining the upper hand. He rolled Kathleen so she was on the bottom and pinned her to the floor with his weight. As soon as he did, Mace raised his hands and a blast of fire shot out and hit the wolf in the back.

"You dare to take my mate," Mace snarled as the alpha roared and rolled off Kathleen. His shirt was burned and his back was blistering already.

The alpha stared at Mace in surprise as he climbed to his feet and faced them. As he did, Kathleen crawled away and used the wall to get herself in a sitting position. Tabby took that moment to race around the edge of the room and drop beside Kathleen. She gathered the wolf close as she watched to see what the Fallen would do.

"Do you know what we are?" Mace roared as he took a step towards the alpha.

"I have no goddamned idea," the alpha sneered. "But you've interrupted my mating, and for that I will gut you."

Mace threw back his head and laughed, causing the alpha to rear back in anger.

"You took the mate of a Fallen," Mace smirked. "You think you can kill me, have at it."

Then Mace opened his arms and taunted the alpha when he crooked his finger in invitation. The alpha snarled and leaped, shifting at the last minute in mid air. Mace flipped over his palm and shot another ball of fire at the alpha, hitting him in the chest. The alpha howled in pain and dropped to the floor.

When Tabby looked at Killian, it was to see him leaning against the door frame with his arms crossed. He seemed amused if the smirk on his face was any indication. She turned back to see the alpha once more climbing to his feet and leaping at Mace. Again a ball of fire shot at the wolf, and it caught him in the shoulder.

The wolf slammed into the ground, but this time he shifted back as he did so. It was clear the alpha was badly hurt, as he didn't rise and leap again. Instead he turned pained eyes on Kathleen.

"Why would you choose a Fallen over a wolf?" he demanded.

Kathleen slowly rose and immediately Tabby let go and assisted her. When they were standing, Kathleen moved right across the room to Mace, and Tabby moved to Killian.

"Because Mace is worth fighting for," Kathleen declared as she curled into his side. "He's strong, he's gorgeous, and he's everything to me." Then she looked up at Mace with stars in her eyes. "Please get me out of here," she demanded.

Mace took a minute to wipe a smear of blood off Kathleen's cheek, then he bent down and scooped her up. The sight of the small wolf held so preciously by the giant man caused a tear to slip from Tabby's eye. She was happy they'd gotten to her in time. The couple moved down the stairs and Killian took Tabby's hand, pulling her after them.

"What about the alpha?" she asked, but when she turned back to look at him, his eyes were closed and it was clear he had passed out.

"The Enforcers can deal with him," Killian grunted. "Right now all Mace is interested in is taking care of his girl."

Tabby nodded. "Do you think she's hurt bad?"

"Kathleen's a wolf Kitten. She has some scratches, but they'll be gone within the hour," Killian assured her.

Tabby smiled, then squealed when he picked her up and strode down the hall.

Chapter 36
Killian

When Killian stepped outside the sight that greeted them was horrific. Blood covered the ground, and moans of pain emanated from the bodies that still had life flowing through them. The Enforcers were dealing with the wounded wolves, but all their heads turned as the four came into their line of sight. Cade was the first to stand and approach them.

"Mace, good to see you got your mate," he grinned in greeting. Then he turned to Kathleen. "I'm sorry things got so bad. If the council had known they would have done something about it."

Kathleen nodded in understanding as Mace set her on her feet. "That's my fault," she admitted. "I thought I could handle it myself. I honestly didn't think my father would hand me over. And when he did there was no way to let Mace know." She smiled up at Mace then. "But he came for me anyway. And just in time too."

Mace growled as he grabbed her waist and pulled her tight against his chest. "It was damn close. You put up a good fight though. I'll be damn proud to have you mated to me properly. And that's getting done tonight," he declared.

She laughed then. "You'll get no arguments from me. I can't wait to be yours. It's all I wish for."

Killian grinned when Mace leaned down and slammed his lips against hers. It was a show of possession, and it warmed his heart to see everything work out the way it should for his friend. He hated to think what would have happened had they been just a few minutes later.

"Jesus, can you keep it PG," Shane complained as he placed his hands over his eyes. "Unmated wolf here. I don't need to see that."

The group chuckled, but Mace just raised his hand and gave Shane the middle finger as he continued to kiss his girl. He knew Shane was only saying that to release the tension. The wolf was extremely good at doing that sort of thing.

"Did he kill the alpha?" James questioned as he stepped up beside Cade. The wolf watched the couple with a small smile on his face. James had gone through some terrible times with his own mate, and he was open about showing his happiness when others got mates of their own.

"No," Killian explained as he let Mace have his moment. "He's unconscious and he's badly hurt, but he isn't dead."

Surprised, James looked back at Mace. "I would have killed him. I'm surprised you could walk out with the alpha still breathing."

"Kathleen was his priority," Killian answered for Mace. "When she decided she wanted out of there, Mace picked her up and didn't even spare the alpha another thought."

"Right," James replied. "I'll go in and get him."

"I'll go with you," Shane sighed. "Those two aren't going to stop anytime soon and my retinas are burning."

Paul was watching the couple as well, but he had a sad look on his face. Killian knew the wolf had met his mate years ago, but due to her age and the circumstances, he couldn't claim her. He felt for him and hoped the two would be reunited soon.

"I'll go too," Paul declared as he turned away and strode after them.

Killian glanced around, unsure of what he should do. His Kitten was sticking close, and it was a relief. He was glad she was still in the mood to listen, and wasn't insisting on doing anything to put her in harms way.

"Just keep your eyes on the rest of the wounded. They're scattered around and I don't want any of them getting up," Cade requested. "I need to take a minute to call the council. We need instructions on what to do with the pack, and both alpha's need to be dealt with."

"Right," Killian grunted as he moved to a small group of wounded and looked at them. They were all in rough shape, and it didn't look like they could move let alone stand and fight again. He knew Cade was only asking him to do this so he could keep Tabby close. He appreciated the wolf's understanding of his needs.

A minute later the three wolves came flying back out of the main doors to the pack house.

"The alpha's gone," James yelled as he shifted and sniffed the air.

"Keep the girls close," Cade ordered. "He won't be far, and he'll want revenge."

Mace was still wrapped around Kathleen, so they weren't a problem, but Tabby was two steps away from him and it was two steps too far. One of the wounded suddenly jumped to his feet right beside her and gave her a hard shove. At the same time the alpha came flying out of a lower window, sending broken glass in every direction. Killian roared as he moved, but he knew that shove had pushed her closer to the alpha. There was no way he was going to reach her in time.

Chapter 37
Tabby

Tabby eyed the wounded wolves on the ground. The battle had been a bloodbath, and the wolves hadn't stood a chance. The Enforcers and the Fallen were brutal in their attack, and they took down the pack quickly.

She watched as Mace and Kathleen stood close together. He had his arms around her and he was whispering in her ear. The small smile on the girl's face clearly showed how much she liked his whatever he was saying. Tabby was happy for them. She knew things could have turned out badly for the couple.

Tabby glanced back at Killian and found his eyes on her. She knew she wasn't the angel that the prophecy mentioned, and that they weren't made for each other, but she didn't care anymore. She was his. She knew it in her heart. She wouldn't fight him anymore on that. She would accept the time she had with him and not take it for granted.

Tabby went to take one step towards him when he paled. A look of horror came over his face, and it caused terror to course through her veins. The wolf on the ground beside her leaped up, and she didn't even have a second to react. He slammed both his hands right in the middle of her chest and gave her a mighty shove. The push was so forceful that she flew back, right into the arms of the alpha.

Killian was moving towards her, and she knew Mace and all the Enforcers were moving as well, but she kept her eyes on her Fallen. The alpha wrapped one powerful arm around her upper shoulders and she was trapped tight against his chest. Tears streamed down her face as she knew her ending had come.

The alpha lifted his hands, and claws sprouted from his fingernails. The sight was horrifying and Tabby quickly looked away and back to Killian. He was almost to her when the alpha slammed his claws into her chest. The pain was excruciating, and if the alpha hadn't had such a tight grip on her she would have fallen. Blood flowed from the gaping hole he'd made as he violently ripped his claws back out.

She stood frozen, disbelief and pain showing clearly on her face. Black spots danced before her eyes as she tried to stay focused on Killian. Then the alpha was torn from her and she was free. Losing his arms caused her to sway, and then the ground was rushing up towards her as she collapsed.

She waited for more pain, but it never came. Killian was there, and he slid across the dirt to land under her. His warm strong body cushioned her fall. Then she was on her back and encased in his arms. He spread his legs, and she found herself cradled against his chest. She looked up, and the devastation on Killian's face hurt more than her wound.

"Killian," she rasped as a trickle of blood rose up her throat and choked her. She coughed as it dripped from her mouth and ran down her chin.

"I've got you Kitten. Hold on for me," he growled at her.

Tabby blinked up at him, then looked around. All the Enforcers, along with Mace and Kathleen, were standing close. And they all had various expressions of pain on their faces.

"It's okay," Tabby choked out as she tried to reassure them. "It doesn't even hurt anymore." And she realized it didn't. The pain was fading and a calmness was coming over her.

Tears flowed down Killian's face as she looked back at him, his tough facade slipping. She desperately wanted to wipe them away, but she found she couldn't lift her arm.

"The alpha?" she questioned him.

"Dead," James rumbled, and she rolled her eyes to look at him. It was getting too hard to move her head. "I took his head."

She tried to smile at the Enforcer, but his raised brow let her know it didn't quite work. She was getting cold and there was a pressure on her chest. When she looked down, she saw Killian had both his hands there, and he was shouting for the rest of them to help him.

"There's nothing we can do," Cade sorrowfully imparted. "The wound is too serious. Even with her healing ability, it's too late."

She knew that too, but she had too much blood in her mouth to tell him that. She swallowed and swallowed, desperate to get one more thing out.

"I love you," she whispered to Killian as she felt herself slip away.

The blood came up again, and it felt like she was drowning. She lost all feeling in her body and mourned that she couldn't feel his arms anymore. She also couldn't hear. Killian was yelling at her, but she had absolutely no idea what he was saying. Then her world turned black, and she lost his beautiful eyes.

Her last thought as she drifted away was that she hoped the prophecy was true. She wanted Killian to find the love he was meant to, because she now knew for sure it hadn't been meant for her.

Chapter 38
Killian

Killian knew his beautiful Kitten was dead, but he refused to believe it. She had the ability to heal. She would come back to him. He carefully placed her on the ground and used the bottom of his shirt to wipe at the blood coating her mouth. Then he leaned down, tilted her head back, and blew his own breath into her mouth. After a minute, he reared back and started chest compressions. He did thirty before he again tilted her head back and blew into her mouth once more.

"Killian, stop," Mace gently ordered as he placed a hand on his shoulder.

Killian knocked his hand away and ignored him. His Kitten would come back. He just had to help her. He continued pushing on her chest, then once more leaned over and blew air into her mouth. He could feel her skin getting colder, but he pushed it to the back of his mind.

"She's immortal. She'll come back," Killian roared at the group.

"She can only heal. Death is something she can't come back from," Cade patiently tried to explain.

"She's not fucking dead," Killian roared back.

Then Kathleen dropped to her knees beside him. She placed her tiny hand on his face and forced him to look at her. Tears ran down her face and she was extremely pale.

"Please Killian," she begged. "Her wound is too bad. He ripped her chest open. She's gone. It's time to stop." Then she broke down and Mace was there lifting her to her feet. He wrapped her up in his arms and nodded at Killian in agreement.

"She can't be gone. It can't end like this," Killian painfully whispered as his shoulders dropped and he hung his head. "She was meant for me."

"Maybe the prophecy was right," Shane hedged. "Maybe she wasn't meant to be yours."

Killian slowly turned to face the Enforcer with a look of pure rage on his face. He pushed to his feet and the ass backed up.

"You want to say that again," Killian growled as he moved towards Shane. "That beautiful broken girl was mine. I don't give a fuck what a stupid piece of paper says. I loved her." He slammed his fist against his heart and roared. "I felt it in here."

Shane raised his hands in surrender, but Killian was beyond caring. "I'm sorry man," Shane acknowledged as he backtracked. "I shouldn't have said that."

"You fucking think," Killian shouted as he kept advancing. He was within hitting distance when Cade stepped in front of him.

"We all know Shane speaks before he thinks," Cade interjected. "The guys an ass." When Shane went to argue, Cade held up his hand and stopped him. "But he's a damn fine Enforcer, and once he finds his own mate he'll change his tune."

"How the hell am I supposed to live without her?" Killian questioned as he turned his attention away from Shane and placed it on Cade.

"You don't," James answered for him. "You live each day hoping it's your last, and you think about her every minute. You don't live. You become a shell and just go on. And you dream of the day your miserable existence ends and you're reunited in death."

"But you got your mate back. That wasn't the end for you," Killian pointed out.

"Then you believe. And you pray that the same happens for you my friend," James responded.

Killian turned back to Tabby, but his love was definitely gone. There wasn't a speck of life in her. He clung to James' words, but they seemed unrealistic as he stared at her.

Killian took a step towards her, but a strong wind shoved him back. He glanced to the others to see their expressions of confusion as they too were forced back. Calling on his strength he dropped his shoulders, braced his legs, and forced his massive body to take another step. As he did so, the wind got stronger and it threw him back at least ten feet before he could stop.

Then Killian heard a flapping sound, and he understood. He looked up and there he was, Azriel, the Angel that had put the hit out on his Kitten. He glared at the Angel as he battled the wind, but no matter how much he pushed, he couldn't move closer.

"Don't you touch her you miserable piece of filth," he yelled at his old friend. But Azriel remained silent as his feet landed on the ground.

The Angel took a minute to regard him, then he leaned down and picked up Tabby. Her lifeless body hung limply from his strong arms. Killian called on all the power he had, but the wind continued to blow. He was helpless and all he could do was watch, as Azriel flapped his giant white wings and soared up into the air.

Roaring in anger Killian knelt, then used his strength to push himself up. He leaped high, but Azriel was already out of reach. Azriel looked down at him as he flew higher into the sky and disappeared into the clouds. The last thing Killian saw was a look of determination on the Angel's normally blank face.

Chapter 39
Azriel

Azriel sat on the edge of his desk and crossed his arms. His entire focus was on the stunning girl lying on his couch. She was a beautiful thing, and not just in looks. The girl had a quick wit and a fire inside that would appeal to any man. He knew she also had a sweet side, and he understood how Killian had fallen for her after one look. The Angel actually felt a touch of jealousy for his friend. The white dress someone had placed her in gave her an air of innocence that called to him.

The girl's fingers were twitching, a sure sign she was about to wake. Her breathing was steady, and he watched as her chest rode and fell. A stray lock of hair fell over one side of her face, and he ached with the need to stay where he was. She wasn't his and brushing it away would show an intimacy he didn't have with her.

As he continued to watch, Tabby slowly opened her eyes. She blinked several times, and then confusion clouded her features. She sat up quickly, and the poor girl almost gave herself whiplash as she twisted her head in every direction to take in her surroundings. When she noticed him her eyes narrowed and she scowled at him.

"You," Tabby spat as she gripped the couch so tight her knuckles turned white.

"Me," he replied as innocently as he could. Then he couldn't stop the grin that spread across his face.

"Where the hell am I?" she demanded.

"You're in my office," Azriel replied as his smile grew bigger.

She huffed at him, and he had had to bite back his laugh. The girl was fun when she was riled.

"Killian was right," Tabby hissed. "You're an ass."

That comment wiped the smile from his face. He dropped his arms and pushed away from the desk, then glared back at her.

"I'm no such thing," Azriel growled back.

"I died. You carted me off to heaven didn't you?" Tabby questioned.

Azriel shrugged his shoulders. "Isn't that what happens when you die?"

"So you bring all the dead to your office?" Tabby asked with a hint of snark.

"Only the important ones," Azriel shot back at her.

He knew she didn't like his answer when her pretty little cheeks turned bright red and her brows rose. She took a step towards him, and then she ran at him. As soon as she did brilliant white wings sprouted from her back and lifted her off the ground. An ear-splitting scream had him cringing and covering his ears as a look of horror crossed her face.

"Azriel," she cried in a complete panic. Her little arms and legs were flailing as her wings continued to keep her afloat.

Sighing, he strode across the room, grabbed her around the waist and pulled her down. As soon as her feet touched the ground she hauled back her arm and punched him in the chin. He staggered back, surprised by the strength her tiny frame had hidden.

"I'm an Angel?" Tabby then roared in his ear.

Azriel rubbed his sore jaw and shrugged his shoulders. He had no idea how to respond. He was worried she would hit him again, so he thought it best to remain silent. When she scrutinized the objects on his desk with a mischievous glint in her eye, he dropped his hand and gave her his best authoritative look.

"Don't you dare," Azriel growled at her, but it was too late. She grabbed a paperweight and launched it at his head. He barely had time to duck before a stapler followed it. He knew then he had been wrong in his assessment of her. There was no sweet in her at all. The girl was all hellfire.

"Fucking stop," Azriel bellowed as a book nailed him in the chest.

"I don't want to be here," Tabby screamed as she ripped out his keyboard and held it over her head. "I want to be back with Killian."

Azriel couldn't help himself, even with his stinging chest and throbbing jaw, he threw back his head and laughed. Stunned, Tabby dropped the keyboard and watched him with wide eyes. It took him about a minute to get a hold of himself. And when he did, he had to wipe the tears from his eyes. The girl was a riot.

"Why didn't you say that?" Azriel asked her with a touch of tenderness in his voice. When she blinked at him he winked back at her. Immediately the confusion cleared and a huge grin appeared.

"You truly are a good friend," Tabby declared.

He smirked back at her, but he had no rebuttal. He really was.

Chapter 40
Killian

Killian was losing his ever loving mind. His Kitten was gone, dead and carried away by Azriel, and he wasn't handling it well. He was drinking, he was fighting, and he had four damned Enforcers following him around. It had been a week now, and he was sick of it.

Killian was in yet another bar, and a half full bottle of whiskey was sitting in front of him. He'd forgone the glass and was now swigging directly from the bottle. James was his babysitter today, and the wolf was eyeing him with a look of trepidation.

Of all the Enforcers, James was the one he related to the most. He was quieter than the rest, and he understood what he was going through. James didn't fight him when he drank too much, and he even backed him up in some of the fights Killian had started.

When James turned to him and sighed, he knew the Enforcer was done with the silent treatment. He set the bottle down he had just taken a healthy swig from, and turned on his stool. When they were eye to eye, Killian lifted his hand and gave a quick flick of his wrist, signalling James to get on with it.

"You loved her," James stated, and Killian glared back at him.

"You think?" he growled back, stunned that James would start with that. "You know I fucking did."

James held up his hand and Killian shut up. He was pissed, but being a Fallen the liquor didn't affect him, so he was curious to see where the Enforcer was headed with this shit.

"She was your true mate. You're absolutely sure of that?" James pushed.

"For god's sake, yes," Killian grunted. "She was mine. I knew it and she knew it. I don't care what the damn prophecy said. She was my mate. Now she's gone and I want no one else."

"So you're ignoring the prophecy," James stated. "You're not willing to find the Angel it mentioned and try to love again. She may be the mate you thought Tabby was."

"No," Killian responded as he stared the Enforcer down. "And you're a dick for even suggesting that. You think of finding another when you thought your mate was dead?"

James straightened on his chair and anger radiated off him. "No," he growled back.

"Exactly," Killian sneered. "So stop. You're out of fucking line."

"Right," James agreed. "But bear with me for a minute." Killian studied the Enforcer, and figured the wolf would say what he had to regardless of Killian's attitude.

"I assume you got a point in asking me this shit?" Killian demanded. "Because I don't like this line of questioning."

"I do," James replied, as Cade, Paul and Shane stepped into the bar. James nodded at him and remained silent until the rest had joined them.

"What the fuck do you need to say that you had to wait for backup before you told me?" Killian huffed. "You think I'm going to go ballistic?" James sighed again and Killian narrowed his eyes.

"There's a good possibility," James finally grunted.

Killian eyed the rest of the Enforcers, but they all looked on with hard looks. It was clear they were ready to fight, so whatever James was about to tell him was going to set him off.

"Spit if out," Killian ordered.

"Azriel has been a good friend to you in the past?" James questioned.

"Until recently, I considered him one," Killian agreed. "But not anymore. The next time I see him I'm taking his head."

James nodded. "I'd do the same, but a week has passed and we've been talking," James continued as he motioned to the others. "We think Azriel did what he did because he had a reason. We think the Angel was trying to help."

"You care to elaborate on that," Killian demanded. His heart was racing and his head was pounding. It was obvious the Enforcers had figured out something important, but Killian was afraid to hope.

"Jesus you're not good at spitting things out," Shane huffed as he pushed in front of James and glared at him.

"I'm doing it carefully," James replied. "I'm considering Killian's feelings."

"We don't have time for feelings," Shane argued. Then he turned back to Killian. "We think Azriel was trying to kill her because she's the Angel from the prophecy. You saving her fucked that up, and he's trying to rectify that mistake. He knows she's your mate, but because of your feelings for her, you'll never kill her. He's been trying to save you that pain and fulfil the prophecy at the same time."

Killian stared at the Enforcer for a full minute before he lost it. "God damn it," he roared as he picked up the bottle of whiskey and threw it across the bar. The entire place went silent as everyone in it turned their eyes on him, but he didn't care. Before anyone could blink he was off the stool and flying out the door. When he reached the parking lot, he stopped and glared up at the sky.

"Azriel, you get your miserable little ass down here," he bellowed loud enough to rattle the windows of the cars surrounding him, and set off several alarms.

The Enforcer's had followed him out of the bar, and of course Shane had to get in one last thing.

"And the fun begins," the Enforcer declared as he leaned against the brick wall of the bar and crossed his arms across his massive chest. Then he had the audacity to wink at Killian.

Chapter 41
Tabby

Tabby paced the room as she tried to figure out what to do. It looked like Azriel had done everything he had to help them, and it was a huge relief to her. All she wanted now was to get back down to Killian.

"You do realize they chose you to to be a White Angel," Azriel told her. "Only a few are hand picked for that position."

Tabby stopped her pacing and turned to him in surprise. "So I should be honoured?" she asked sarcastically.

"You should," Azriel agreed with a small smile.

"And what is a White Angel?" Tabby questioned him.

"It means you help the very young pass over. You would be making the transition for babies easier. The young don't understand what is happening to them. You provide the comfort they need," Azriel explained.

Tabby placed her hands on her hips. "So you're trying to talk me into staying?"

Azriel shook his head. "Definitely not. I just want you to understand that you are more than what you think you are. You are the Angel in the prophecy, and you were meant to be with Killian. You deserve happiness. But also understand they chose you for your strength. You aren't one to fold when things get tough. You're the type to grab a sword and fight by your mates side."

Tabby reached up and swiped at a stray tear that rolled down her face. Azriel's words were powerful, and exactly what she needed to hear. She squared her shoulders and moved to his side.

"Thank you," Tabby replied. She would have said more, but Azriel suddenly covered his ears and cringed.

"Shit," Azriel cursed as he removed his hands and shook his head. As soon as he did he was cringing again and placing them right back over his ears.

"What's the matter?" Tabby questioned as she looked up at him in concern.

"Your goddamned man is yelling in my ear," Azriel sneered. "I have a feeling he's mourned enough and wants an explanation. Either that, he's figured out what I'm doing and he's pissed."

"I'll go with pissed," she grinned as he glared back at her. "So how do I get back to him?"

Azriel lowered his arms and looked at her sympathetically. "You fall."

Tabby eyed him with a raised brow. "So you take my wings and I plunge to earth like Killian did?" she questioned warily.

"No," Azriel responded. "You did nothing wrong. If I take your wings without reason, I'll be damning myself too. This has to be your decision alone."

"But then how do I fall?" Tabby pushed nervously. She knew there had to be a way to do it, she just had a feeling she wouldn't like it.

"I go down and deal with your mate so you're alone. You go into the top drawer of my desk, take out the knife you'll find in there, and cut the wings off yourself," Azriel explained.

Tabby paled. "I knew I wouldn't like what you had to say."

"I'm sorry honey," Azriel sympathized. And it relieved her to see he actually looked upset. "It's not something I'd wish on my worst enemy. Are you sure you want to do this?"

"I love him," Tabby told him honestly. "I'd go to hell and back for him."

Azriel visibly shuddered and then leaned down so they were eye level. "And that's exactly what it will feel like. Be strong Tabitha, and I'll see you soon."

Then he brushed his lips against her forehead and disappeared. The room felt colder without him in it with her, but it may have been the fear coursing through her body. She was terrified, and she was shaking like a leaf, but she was also extremely determined.

Without wasting a minute or taking the time to think, she hurried over to the desk and opened the drawer. Sitting on a piece of folded up cloth was the knife, just as Azriel had promised. She picked it up and held it in her hand. It was heavy and felt cold, but the blade looked sharp and deadly.

Tabby took several deep breaths in an attempt to calm herself, then she knelt on the floor. It would hurt, and she didn't want to be standing in case she passed out. Bravely, she reached back with her right hand and grabbed hold of her left wing. Then she awkwardly swung her left arm over her shoulder and sliced through the wing.

The pain hit instantly, and she dropped to all fours and closed her eyes. Vomit rushed up her throat and she had to fight it back. She could feel warm blood rushing from the wound to coat her back and she couldn't even scream. She was afraid she'd throw up as soon as she opened her mouth.

When she was sure she could continue, she switched hands with the knife, and did the same thing with the other wing. As soon as it was done a blinding white light filled the room, and she was falling. This time though the scream was ripped from her throat, and she felt like blades of ice were tearing through her body as the wind rushed over her.

Chapter 42
Killian

Killian paced the parking lot as he continued to roar for Azriel. He knew the Angel could hear him, so it was only a matter of time before he showed. And the longer the Angel took to come down, the longer Killian had to feed his rage. At this point he was ready to knock Azriel on his ass without even hearing his explanation.

Cade and the other Enforcers had felt it necessary to clear out the bar and the surrounding area. Now they leaned against the wall. They looked on casually, but Killian could see they were ready to step in if he needed them. He just hoped they remained on his side.

The large gust of wind was the first indication that Azriel had arrived. Killian bent his knees and braced, not wanting to be pushed back this time. The flapping noise followed, and that got to him. Some days he missed his wings, and today was one of those days. He would have liked to fight on equal footing, high above the clouds where they were meant to be. There was nothing like gliding on the wind while locked in a deadly battle.

As soon as the Angel's feet touched the ground, Killian charged him. He raised his arm as he moved, and just as Azriel lifted his head, Killian nailed him. His fist was like a hammer, and with his whole body behind it, it threw his old friend across the lot. Azriel dug in, and the pavement split as he slid, but he was a good twenty feet back when he finally stopped. When he lifted a hand to rub his chin, Killian smirked at him.

"Seriously," Azriel cursed. "I think you're getting stronger."

"Nah," Killian sneered. "Just got a lot of anger inside me. Emotions fuel the fire."

Azriel frowned at him. "Well calm that fire. I'm not in the mood to fight you."

"And I don't give a fuck," Killian retorted. "If you expected me to smile and say thank you, you shouldn't have come."

"Can I explain?" Azriel huffed as he raised his arms in surrender.

Killian's answer was to raise his hands, palms out, and blast the Angel. The power that flew at Azriel lifted him off the ground and slammed him into the side of the bar. The wall cracked, bricks crumbled, and Killian gave a satisfied grunt. Azriel slowly pulled from the rubble and made a show of dusting himself off.

"I'd say Killian two, Azriel a big fat zero," Shane chuckled from the side lines.

Azriel frowned at the Enforcer, but Killian grinned back at the wolf. The Enforcer's humour was growing on him.

"You put a kill order out on my girl," Killian snarled as he finally turned his attention back to Azriel.

"Because she needed to die and you wouldn't do it. Her time was up, and the higher ups had plans for her," Azriel sighed. "She's always been meant for more."

"And you had to be the one to see them through?" Killian pushed.

"I didn't trust anyone else," Azriel shrugged.

Killian lifted his hands and blasted the Angel once more. Azriel slammed back into the bricks and groaned in frustration.

"You went after my girl. You got her killed," Killian roared.

"I did what needed to be done so she could be with you. As long as she was alive the two of you didn't stand a chance," Azriel shouted back as he stepped away from the wall.

"She's not fucking here. So how did you help me?" Killian demanded.

"She's an Angel now, so the prophecy can be fulfilled," Azriel shouted.

"I don't give a flying fuck about the prophecy. She's a goddamned Angel now and I'm a Fallen, we don't fit," Killian roared as he started for Azriel once more. "I'm not allowed in Heaven, and she can't stay down here."

"Which is why I gave her a choice," Azriel stated as he stared him in the eye.

Killian froze as he took in what his old friend had said. "What choice?"

"To be with you, or to live her days as a White Angel," Azriel explained.

"Jesus," Killian choked out. "A goddamned White Angel."

"She's special," Azriel shrugged. "And she made her choice."

"But you don't turn down an order. She can't just walk away," Killian replied, not fully understanding.

"No she can't," Azriel calmly agreed. Then he looked up to the sky, drawing Killian's gaze with it.

Killian saw nothing at first, then a small dot caught his attention. It was moving quickly, and it was heading straight for them. As he watched in rapt fascination the dot got larger, and as it did he realized it was human. And that realization made his blood freeze in horror.

"She fell for you," Azriel softly told him. "That brave girl chose you. She will need you now. You understand the pain she's putting her body through."

"Mother fucker," Killian roared, then he leaped and headed straight for her.

Chapter 43
Tabby

Tabby knew the earth had to be getting close. The fall had seemed never ending, and the pain had caused her to black out several times. It never lasted long though. She'd wake again to what felt like knives of ice slicing through her back. She assumed it was the rush of cold wind putting pressure on the open wounds from her wings. The loud rush of wind was getting louder and Tabby feared for her ear drums. She had stopped screaming and had forced her body to relax, letting gravity guide her down.

Tabby could think of nothing but Killian during her fall. She wanted to hear his voice once more. She wanted to touch him. And she wanted him to wrap his massive arms around her and never let go. She understood everything now. She was the Angel from the prophecy. When Killian saved her he changed their fate, and Azriel had taken it upon himself to see it got back on track. She couldn't say she agreed with Ariel's methods, putting a kill order on her was a little extreme, but she appreciated his reasons.

Tabby could hear traffic now, it was distant, but unmistakable. She closed her eyes, crossed her arms over her chest, and breathed deeply. Because of the pain she was experiencing, she knew when she slammed into the ground it would feel like hitting a brick wall. She had no idea how she'd ever be able to get back up again. But Killian and Mace had both survived their falls. So she knew she could as well.

All the noises were blurring together now, the wind, the traffic, and the roar of her heart, but something was rising above it. Tabby tried to clear her mind and pick up on that one noise. It almost sounded like a bellow. Her whole body tensed as she listened closer. It was getting louder, and it was clearly a bellow. She had a feeling she knew exactly who belonged to that bellow. Azriel had left because Killian had been demanding to see him, she had no doubt Killian had found out what she had done.

The bellow turned into a roar, and Tabby caught her name. Tears streamed down her face. She wanted Killian. She needed Killian and he was here. Her body slammed into something and she screamed, terrified it was the ground. But it was warm and comforting. Immediately she opened her eyes and stared into Killian's intense ones. He had her, and he'd locked his arms tight around her. She curled her arms around his shoulders and shoved her face in his neck, breathing in his smell. They were still falling, but she didn't care. She trusted him to see her down safely.

When they hit the ground he took the brunt of the fall, going down on one knee and wrapping himself protectively around her. She was barely jarred, but she heard the crack of the cement below them and saw the cloud of dust that swirled all around them. She kept her hold on him though, refusing to move from the one place she dreamed of being again.

"Kitten," Killian rumbled in his deep timber, ripping a sob from her throat.

"Killian," she whispered back as she dug her nails in his shoulders. "You came to me."

"No Kitten," he growled. "You came to me."

She grinned through her tears, and a blush coated her skin.

"I couldn't stay up there when you were down here," Tabby admitted.

Killian studied her as he tenderly brushed her hair off her face.

"You fell for me," Killian rumbled.

"Well you did it first," she countered. "You lost your wings because you saved me."

"I think we're quite a pair," he finally chuckled, and Tabby relaxed.

"I think we are," she agreed. Then she grew serious as she gripped him tighter. "I'm your mate."

"You were always my mate," Killian countered. "I not once thought you weren't, even when everyone tried to convince me otherwise."

"That's true," Tabby grinned as her tears continued to flow. "I love you Killian."

"I love you too Kitten," Killian growled.

"Jesus Christ, it's only been a couple days," Shane complained as he came to stand beside them.

There was a smacking sound, and when Tabby looked up she saw Shane rubbing the back of his head. He was frowning at Cade, who was standing behind him. Then Azriel was there, bending down and placing his hand on Killian's shoulder.

"I'm sorry about everything," the Angel stated, clearly looking remorseful. Killian nodded, but didn't turn to look at him. Instead he kept his eyes on her.

"It will take me a while to forgive you," Killian told him. "And I don't know if we'll ever get back to the friendship we once shared."

Azriel dropped his head and said nothing more. He removed his hand, stepped back, and leaped. As Tabby watched, his wings unfolded and carried him high into the sky. It was something she swore she'd never tire of seeing.

"Do you miss them?" Killian questioned, and she could feel his body tense as he waited for her to answer. She knew he was asking about her wings.

"God no," Tabby frowned. "I'm too much of a badass now to be an Angel."

"You mean you want your squirt guns back?" James chuckled, and she turned a smile his way.

"No, she wants her sword back," Paul added.

"Blades," Cade threw out. "She's good with her blades."

"Ninja throwing stars," Tabby interrupted. "I'd really like to try those."

Then she stared in wonder as Killian and all the Enforcers threw back their heads and laughed. She was still in pain, but the love and happiness she was feeling overshadowed it.

"I can teach you how to throw fire," Killian told her as his laughter died down.

She could only blink up at him as she took in what he said. Then she dropped her arms and looked down at her hands.

"Run Shane," Tabby warned, but Killian was shaking his head as he stood and carried her away. All she could do was wave at the others, as Killian powered across the parking lot.

Chapter 44
Killian

Killian strode across the parking lot with his Kitten cushioned tightly against his chest. His emotions were all over the place and he felt like a walking time bomb. He thought she was dead. He thought she was lost to him forever. He never for a moment considered he'd ever get a second chance with her. Her skin was warm against his. Her breath tickled his neck and he could feel her heartbeat.

Abruptly Killian stopped walking, and she pulled her head back from his neck to look up at him in confusion. He didn't waste another minute. He leaned down and slammed his mouth against her soft one. She relaxed against him and opened hers, allowing him to slip his tongue inside. The taste of her was intoxicating. He deepened the kiss and heard her soft moan. It was everything to him. He would have kissed her earlier, but he wanted to do it without an audience. This was their moment.

The kiss lasted for a long time, and Killian pulled back reluctantly. Tabby's lips were swollen and her eyes were misty, but it was the love he saw in them that choked him up. She was his now, and he wasn't ever letting her go. Anyone that was foolish enough to try to separate them again he'd decimate, no matter who they were.

Killian pushed across the lot once more and headed for the car he had stashed there. After shifting Tabby in his arms, he opened the passenger side and gently set her on the seat. She was smiling up at him as he kissed her head, then he was shutting her door and heading around to his side. Once he had folded himself in he leaned over, snagged her around the waist and dragged her into the middle. The car was old and it was massive, but because of that it didn't have the middle console like the newer models did. With her body snug against his he could relax and start the car.

Cade, Mace, and the rest of the Enforcers were giving him a couple days to spend time with Tabby, and he was grateful. Azriel had promised to call off the kill order, but he wanted to take her some place safe for a while just in case. He definitely wasn't taking any chances with her life.

"How's your back doing Kitten?" Killian questioned her. He knew from experience that the wounds would take a day or two to heal and that they were extremely painful. He could also tell by the way she had angled her body into his she was hurting. She kept her back away from the seat and gave him her weight. Her head slowly lifted and her tired eyes met his intense ones.

"I'm fine," Tabby lied. When he glared at her she huffed and finally told him the truth. "It hurts a lot. When I was falling it felt like shards of ice were hitting it, now it just burns."

Killian nodded. "It's the open wounds. I'll get you someplace safe and look after you. We'll clean them up, put salve on them, and then wrap them. By tonight they will already start to heal over, and within a couple days will be completely gone. All you'll be left with is a pretty nasty scar."

Tabby nodded and laid her head back on his shoulder. He continued down the highway for another fifteen minutes until she spoke again.

"Where do we go from here?" Tabby asked quietly. Killian leaned over and swiped at a piece of hair he noticed drop across her face.

"I've got some plans, but I don't want to say anything until I've got something finalized. Unless you want to go home, maybe see your dad or any friends you left behind."

"No," she admitted. "It's time my dad figured out his problems on his own. He never acted like a dad with me, so it won't be upsetting if I don't see him again. And I didn't have many friends."

"I'm sorry Kitten," Killian told her. "I find that odd since you've made so many new ones since I've met you."

"Your friends are easy to get close to. They're like funny, protective teddy bears," Tabby declared.

Killian couldn't help but snort at that description. "Don't let any of them hear you call them that. I don't think teddy bears is how they want to be known."

"Badass teddy bears?" Tabby questioned on a grin.

Killian grinned back but didn't respond. Ten more minutes passed when he thought of something else.

"There's a diner just ahead, you hungry?" he asked.

"Not really," Tabby replied. "Besides my dress is torn from the wind and it's covered in blood. I think if I went in people would run out screaming."

Killian growled, not liking that response. "I could go in and grab something?"

"No, honestly I'm just really tired. I want to get cleaned up and then sleep for a week," she admitted.

Killian completely understood, and sleep would definitely speed up the recovery process. He maneuvered over to the side of the road, threw the car in park, then turned towards her. In only a minute he had her laying on the seat with her head in his lap. He snagged a blanket from the back and draped it over her. As he pulled back out on the road, he gently ran his fingers through her hair.

"Sleep Kitten, and when you wake we'll be somewhere with a bed. We'll get you cleaned up and then I'll be able to hold you properly."

She was half asleep already, but mumbled some unintelligible reply as she closed her eyes. Killian was happy to see she didn't even make it another minute before her body relaxed and light snores filled the car.

Chapter 45
Tabby

Tabby woke in a good mood. The car had stopped, and she was still curled up on the seat with her head in Killian's lap. She thought it was the perfect way to wake up, until she heard the loud rattle. She squeezed her eyes shut even tighter and refused to move.

"I'm not getting out," she complained with a sneer.

"Why not?" Killian questioned, and she could hear the smile in his voice. Damn man.

"I know that rattle," she practically growled. "It's those goddamned bones." When Killian chuckled her eyes snapped open.

"They scare off anyone foolish enough to get close," he explained.

"Yeah me," she countered.

Before she could say more he had his door open and was climbing out. She stayed right where she was and gave him the stink eye. He ignored her and reached in to drag her across the seat. Then she was in his arms and they were headed for the hut from hell. She really had high hopes she'd never see this place again.

"I hate it here," Tabby felt the need to inform him.

"I know Kitten, but until everyone knows the kill order is off, this is the safest place for us."

She sighed, knowing he was still worried about that.

"Fine," she huffed. "But I want it known I don't like it."

"Noted," Killian immediately replied. "Besides you're here with me, not Mace. I can guarantee this time will be much more enjoyable."

When Tabby looked up at him his eyes were shining. She could see how happy he was. She pushed the bone wind chimes to the back of her mind and softened her voice.

"Okay," Tabby whispered.

"Okay," Killian repeated. Then he was moving up the steps and kicking open the rickety door. As soon as he entered he headed straight for the bed and laid her down.

"I can't look at that blood anymore. The white dress is covered in it and it's setting me off," he growled. "I'll start the shower and heat the water, then come back and get you."

Tabby nodded in agreement as she shifted to her side. Her back still hurt, but it wasn't as bad as it had been earlier. She took that as a good sign. Killian leaned down, wrapped his hand around her neck, and gave her a slow sensual kiss. It wasn't nearly as intense as the first one had been. This time he took his time and gentled his movements. It was a kiss that made her feel loved.

When he pulled away Tabby whined at the loss of him. The ass smirked at her as he turned on his heal and headed for the bathroom. She listened to the sound of the water being turned on, and his soft footsteps as he moved around the tiny bathroom. Already disliking the fact she couldn't see him, she carefully slid off the bed and stood.

Padding across the floor, Tabby pushed open the bathroom door and leaned against the doorframe. Killian had no idea she was there. As she watched he toed off his boots and then leaned down and pulled off his socks. Next, he put his arms over his head, grabbed his tee by the back of the neck, and yanked it over his head. It was the purring sound she made that finally caught his attention.

"I heard you when you walked across the floor Kitten," Killian told her. "I thought I said to wait a minute and I'd come get you."

"I couldn't see you," Tabby admitted as she gave him her sad face.

He shook his head, but reached out his arm, snagged her wrist, and pulled her into the bathroom. She grinned as Killian brought her small frame close to his large one. When he let go of her she instinctively raised her hands and placed them on his warm chest. Muscles rippled and his tribal tattoos seemed to brighten as she moved her hands over his skin. He didn't move and let her explore, but when Tabby raised her eyes to Killian's, she found his blazing with a fire that took her breath away.

"I need that blood washed off you," Killian growled as he glanced down to the ruined dress she still wore. "It's setting me off."

Tabby looked down at the offending thing herself and nodded. That seemed to be all Killian needed because he reached down, grabbed it in his massive fists, and tore it right down the middle. Then he was flinging the material out the bathroom door and slamming it shut. She stood there in only her underwear and watched in rapt fascination as he hooked his fingers in the waist of his jeans and shoved them down. Then he stepped in the shower wearing only his boxers.

Tabby looked down at her underwear, then made a show of looking at his boxers, clearly indicating she didn't like it.

"I'm not taking you until your wound is better," Killian forced out through his clenched teeth.

He was standing directly under the hot stream of water, and he had his fists clenched so tight she was afraid he'd draw blood. Slowly she lifted her foot and took a step into the shower, but kept a small distance between them.

"I'm not as sore as I was Killian," Tabby softly told him. "It aches, but it's bearable."

His eyes narrowed as he glared down at her. "You're saying that to push me into doing more. I won't risk hurting you."

Tabby looked up at him, loving the concern, but frustrated that he didn't believe her. Shrugging, and knowing that showing him the wound would be the only way to appease him, she spun around and lifted her long hair off her back. His hiss was the only warning she got before his scorching palms landed on her back.

"It's scabbed over," Killian declared with a hint of confusion in his voice. "It's only been a couple hours. It should still be raw."

His warm hands ghosted over her skin, causing her to shiver. Then she was spun back around and staring at his heated eyes once more.

"I guess your rapid healing abilities are to thank for that," Killian smirked, then his face took on a serious look. "I'm cleaning you, quickly, then I'm taking you to bed," he declared.

Chapter 46
Killian

Killian ran his hands through Tabby's long hair as the spray from the shower head rinsed out the conditioner. Her eyes were closed and she looked utterly relaxed. It was more than obvious she was savouring the attention he was giving her. Steam rose all around them and it felt like they were in their own little bubble. Her face was tipped up towards him and her eyes were closed. It was a position he couldn't ignore.

Killian leaned down and felt her breath whisper across his lips. He took those lips with his own, producing a surprised gasp from her. Not wasting a moment, he took advantage of that gasp, slipping his tongue inside to dance with hers. She met his at the same time she wrapped her arms around his neck and plastered her tiny wet body to his. He groaned into the kiss and deepened it.

Killian had no idea how long the kiss lasted, time always stood still when they were together, but eventually he drew back. The look on her face caused his heart to race. Her head was still tipped back, her eyes were still closed, and she still had a hold of him, but the slight smile that graced her lips told him all he needed to know. Lifting his hand, he traced her lips with his finger, then ran it down between her breasts. His girl shivered from that simple light touch.

Deciding he couldn't take anymore, Killian reached up and shut off the water, then threw back the shower door. He stepped out first, then reached back in, seized his Kitten by the waist and lifted her out. Her surprised giggle barely registered, he was too far gone. He spun with her still in his arms and planted her ass on the bathroom counter. A slight squeal at the cold countertop was her only objection.

"I can't wait," Killian admitted on a near growl as his hands roamed her body. "It feels like I'm on fire. I want you so bad. If you don't want me or you're too sore, say the words now and I'll step away."

"I want you," Tabby whispered back as she raised her hand and settled it on his cheek.

Killian took a minute to gage for himself if she was being truthful, but all he saw was her unmasked desire. Nodding, he went to grab her and take her to the bed, but she leaned away and shook her head at him.

"Here," Tabby whispered. "The bed will rub at my scab and irritate it."

Killian grinned, her logic made sense, and that suited him just fine. He stepped between her splayed legs and cemented his wet body against her own. Her skin was chilled, and tiny goosebumps peppered it.

"Cold?" Killian questioned as he rubbed at her arms to warm her.

In response, she leaned forward and licked at the water dripping from his chest. He hissed from the contact, then leaned down to return the favour. Her nipples were pebbled from the cold and they drew him in. He latched onto one and ran his tongue around it, getting a breathy moan in response. Killian played with it, licking, sucking and biting lightly until switching to the other one to give it the same treatment.

A slight tug on his hair had him pulling away and scanning his girl. Her eyes were half closed, and she was arched back with her free hand splayed on the counter behind her. His eyes wandered down her beautiful body and caught on the wetness leaking from her clit. Killian couldn't resist reaching down and running his finger along the slit. She arched her back even more and made a soft purring noise, eliciting a growl from him in return. Then he stopped teasing and pushed his finger into her tight core. Her wetness sucked him in, and he throbbed with need.

Knowing she was ready for him, Killian took his cock in his hand and lined it up with her entrance. His muscles rippled with the effort it took to force his body to take it slow. He knew he was bigger than most, and he didn't want to cause her any unnecessary pain. She arched as he slid inside and made the sweetest moan when he was fully seated. There was no holding back after that.

Killian grabbed her around the waist, pulled her back up so she was tight against him once more, and let loose. He pulled out until only the tip remained, and slammed back into her again and again knowing it wouldn't be long until he came. She was made for him and seemed to catch onto his intensity and match it with her own. The bathroom filled with the sounds of their bodies slapping together and it was a sound that Killian knew he'd never tire of.

When her body shook, he knew she was close. He moved his finger down between them and rubbed at the tiny bud, eliciting a small cry from her. Then she was detonating, and he could feel her pussy tightening around his cock. The action set off his own release, and his roar drowned out her screams.

Killian refused to let go of her afterwards. He rubbed her lower back and made sure to stay away from her wound. He was softening inside of her, but he knew it would only be a few minutes before he'd be hard again and looking to take her once more. She was an addiction, and one he would happily succumb too.

"I love you Tabitha," Killian uttered, using her real name for the first time.

She lifted her head from where she had laid it against his chest and smiled softly up at him. It surprised him to see her eyes shimmering with tears.

"I love you too Killian," she returned. Then she smirked at him. "See, I told you I was the Angel from the prophecy and your true mate."

Killian stared at her a moment in disbelief, then he threw back his head and laughed. His girl was definitely something else.

Chapter 47
Tabby

Tabby and Killian spent three blissfully uninterrupted days at the hut from hell. They cooked, they talked, and they made love for hours on end. Tabby would have called it a honeymoon if they had been anywhere else.   The bond she felt with Killian grew as they learned new things about each other and explored each other's bodies. It was absolutely magical.

By the third morning Tabby was completely healed, and that meant Killian was a lot easier to deal with. He was growly and tense when she was hurt. A healed wound meant he was easier to live with. By the end of the first day a thick scab had appeared. By the morning of the second day the scab was loose and lifting at the corners. And by the third morning it had fallen off. Tabby was left with a faint scar, so light in fact it was hard to see. It definitely wasn't like Killian's angry looking scar tissue, and for that she was grateful.

Today they were tidying up and getting ready to leave. With no belongings to pack, and the cabin being so small, there wasn't much to do. Within an hour they were standing on the porch and shutting the door.

"What's the matter Kitten?" Killian sighed as he took in her forlorn expression and pulled her against his chest. She wrapped her arms around his back and melted into him, before letting out a sigh of her own.

"I hate this place," she declared, something she knew he was well aware of. "But I will miss it. It's the one place I've felt safe, and it's the only place we've gotten to spend any time together in." Killian nodded, indicating he understood what she meant.

"We'll make a place of our own Kitten, and it won't be in the middle of a goddamned swamp. We'll build a cabin somewhere quiet, a stream will be nearby, and we'll be surrounded by trees."

"No mosquitoes?" she questioned as she smacked at one on her arm.

"No mosquitoes," Killian agreed with a chuckle.

She tilted her head and studied him, trying to figure out what he had up his sleeve.

"It sounds to me like you already have something picked out," Tabby declared. "Do you care to share?"

"Nope," Killian smirked. "It's a plan, but it isn't set in stone yet. I don't want to say until I have it sorted."

"Cryptic," she grinned as she moved away and shot the bones a final glare. "So where to?"

"North," he stated. "We'll travel on our own for a bit, then meet up with Mace and Kathleen."

"You spoke to Mace?" Tabby asked in surprise.

"I did," Killian grinned. "The pair are mates now and have been locked away in their own honeymoon of sorts."

"I'm so happy for them," Tabby announced as she clapped her hands. "So Kathleen isn't returning to her pack?"

"No," Killian sneered. "She refuses to even talk to her father, and I don't know if she could anyway. Cade and the Enforcer's had strict instructions to bring him and his second to the council for a disciplinary hearing. They may be executed for their actions."

Tabby gasped and placed her hand over her heart. "That's harsh," she whispered.

"Not at all," Killian disagreed. "Mates are sacred. It's one of the few things that keep the wolves from losing their humanity. Mates restore balance, and they bring out a softer side that otherwise wouldn't be present. They're a blessing."

Killian's words were powerful, and she knew he was thinking about their own mating. There was no bite involved with theirs, but there was a connection she knew would never be broken. Getting close again, she stood on her tip toes and kissed him. He growled against her lips, then his hands buried in her hair and he was deepening the kiss. It was a claiming kiss and one that had the power to drop her to her knees. Every single time he touched her she felt it deep in her heart. She never should have questioned she was his.

Killian broke away from her and his eyes were intense as he looked down at her. "You're in your head," he grunted.

"I'm sorry," Tabby apologized. "I should have never questioned our bond. I felt it the first time I saw you standing over me in the alley, and it's only grown since then. I was never afraid of you, and that should have clued me in."

"A lot was thrown at you at once, and it was hard for you to process it all. You can't fault yourself for having doubts. Besides, it's in the past now. Don't dwell on things you can't change Kitten."

Tabby nodded and placed her small hand in his much larger one. "Are we walking at a normal pace, or can you teach me how to move like the flash?"

"The flash?" Killian questioned as he chuckled. When she grinned at him he grinned back. "Keep hold of my hand. Concentrate on your legs and push your body. It will take time to get the hang of this, but I promise I won't let go."

"Okay," she agreed. "I can do this."

Then he didn't give her a chance to think about it, his grip on her hand tightened and he took off. She had no choice but to move with him, or risk being dragged the entire way. Tabby ran just as she normally would, but she concentrated on going faster. Her legs picked up speed with each step she took until the trees turned into a blur. It was the most exhilarating experience she'd ever had.

Chapter 48
Killian

Killian was in awe of his Kitten. Instead of panicking and suffering from all she had been through, his girl was embracing it. She easily kept pace with him as he ran through the swamp, and even seemed to enjoy herself. She had a huge smile on her face, and she kept a firm grip on his hand.

When they reached the edge of the swamp Killian slowed their pace to a walk. It was dangerous to run fast when they could be spotted by a local. Azriel had assured him he would call off the kill order, and it had been a couple days, but Killian remained cautious as they left the safety of the swamp. He crossed a main road and headed for the parking lot of an abandoned diner. It's where he had stashed the car, and it would make traveling a hell of a lot faster.

Killian pulled a set of keys out of his front pocket and unlocked the doors. The car was a shit box, but he was in agreement with Tabby's method of picking out cars. The older the car the easier to break into when you needed a fast getaway. Tabby grinned at him, but didn't say a word about it. He could only image on the trip here she wasn't paying much attention to what she was riding in.

Before they could even climb into the car, a growling noise sounded to their right. It caught both their attention, and they twisted to see what had uttered it. It surprised Killian to see a werewolf standing there. He was in human form, except for the deadly claws he had on display, and he looked pissed.

"Mine," the creature sneered as he stared directly at his Kitten.

"Oh for goodness' sake," Tabby huffed as she placed her hands on her hips on glared at the creature. "Not you again?"

Killian turned to her in surprise. "You've run into this one before?" he questioned as he pointed at the wolf.

"When I left the hospital he was waiting by my car. He was the first paranormal to come after me. He said the same thing then too," Tabby admitted.

"And you got away?" Killian questioned with a raised brow.

"I did," she chuckled. "Azriel found me too, so I pitted the two against each other and took off."

"Smart girl," Killian grinned, then he turned back to the creature. "The kill order has been retracted, there's no reason for you to come after her."

The wolf tilted his head and studied Killian, and he realized it didn't matter to the creature. The wolf confirmed it a second later.

"I want her, and I don't give a shit about the kill order," he growled.

"She's already mine," Killian growled back as his eyes darkened and his whole body locked in a deadly stance. "And I protect what's mine."

Killian could see out of the corner of his eye that his Kitten was studying the wolf, and it looked like she was trying to figure something out. She seemed way too relaxed about this entire situation, but he didn't have time to figure out why. The wolf was practically salivating in anticipation of getting his hands on his girl, and he wasn't allowing that.

"I'm a Fallen," Killian furiously informed the wolf. "You don't stand a chance."

The wolf snorted in obvious amusement. "I went up against an Angel and walked away. I can do the same this time. Only now I'll be taking your girl with me."

Tabby suddenly huffed and threw up her arms in frustration, drawing both their attention. "I'm right here," his girl sighed as she narrowed her eyes at the wolf. "I need to be included in this conversation."

"Are you going to come with me willing?" the wolf questioned in obvious surprise.

Tabby rolled her eyes and Killian had to bite back his snort. His girl was definitely up to something.

"No," she denied. "Not even if you were the last man on earth. I belong with Killian. He's extremely good looking, he's an awesome kisser, and he loves me."

Killian outright laughed at what she said, and she turned his way and winked, causing him to laugh harder. His girl was having fun with this.

"Enough," the wolf bellowed, not at all impressed with them.

The creature leaped suddenly, and as he did he shifted. Killian roared and headed right for him, but a ball of fire shot through the air and hit the wolf right in the chest. He was thrown back by the force, and when he slammed into the earth there was a giant hole in his chest. The surrounding skin was singed, and it was clear the ass was dead. Killian looked to his Kitten, more than a little surprised by what she had done.

"How the hell did you figure out how to do that?" Killian questioned.

"I applied the same concept as the running thing to it. I concentrated and pushed. Easy peasy," she shrugged.

"Jesus," he huffed. "I'm glad you're on my side."

She grinned smugly. Then she moved his way, stood on her tiptoes, and took his mouth in a kiss that ensured him she was more than happy about that too.

Chapter 49
Tabby

Killian drove for two days, only stopping for food and sleep. The time went fast, but then it always did when they were together. They talked, they laughed, and they made love until the wee hours of the morning. They grew closer with each passing day.

Luckily there were no further incidents. Killian had explained that Azriel had lifted the kill order, and it appeared he had fallen through. It was a blessing to not be looking over her shoulder all the time, but it was strange after doing it for so long.

They had been traveling through forested hills for about a half hour when Killian slowed and pulled onto what looked like a path through the trees. Tabby immediately undid her seatbelt and leaned forward, placing her palms on the windshield. It was early fall, but already the surrounding trees were awash with bright shades of reds, oranges and yellows. It was utterly breathtaking.

"Where are we?" Tabby questioned as her eyes remained glued on the forest. "This is incredible."

"Somewhere special," Killian cryptically replied, and she could hear the smile in his voice.

When they pulled out into a clearing, she couldn't help the gasp that escaped her as she climbed out of the car. The sight took her breath away it was that beautiful. Trees bowed over the clearing, giving them a canopy like appearance and secluding the area in privacy. A stream ran along the edge of the clearing and the sound of trickling water was soothing. Stunning red cardinal flowers grew amongst the daisy's, giving the whole area a fairy like quality.

Then there was the house. It looked like an old stone cottage, and it fit in with its surroundings perfectly. The cottage itself was one level, and the tin roof and tiny twinkling lights strung up around it added to the enchanted effect. Tabby couldn't take her eyes off it. She could image sleeping in it at night and leaving the windows open so she could fall asleep to the lulling sound of the water.

"What is this?" Tabby questioned as she looked up into Killian's bright eyes. His arms were wrapped tight around her, and she knew he'd been watching her so he wouldn't miss her reaction.

"Home," he replied simply, a grin spreading across his face.

"What?" Tabby asked, not believing what he was saying.

"I've never had a home of my own," Killian admitted. "My whole life I've never found somewhere I wanted to settle, neither have I found anyone I've wanted to share my life with. You've changed all that. I want a family with you. I want to settle and build roots. I want everything with you."

Tabby blinked back tears as she took in all he was saying. "I want that too," she whispered. "Living here with you would be a dream come true. It's something I never imagined I'd ever get to have."

Tabby stood on her tiptoes and framed Killian's face with her hands. That's as far as she got before he leaned down and took her mouth with his. The kiss was full of love and promise and it made her heart swell. When he pulled back a loud cheer rose from the surrounding woods.

Shocked, Tabby peered into the trees to see who was there. When about a dozen people appeared she could only cry in happiness. Mace and Kathleen were the first to emerge, then came Cade with a woman close to his side, and James with a woman of his own. Paul, Shane and several other Enforcers followed them, along with more she recognized, but didn't know by name.

Tabby laughed through her tears as Kathleen reached her and they embraced. She didn't know the girl well, but she was thrilled to see her.

"What are you doing here?" Tabby questioned her new friend.

Kathleen grinned as she turned and pointed into the trees. "Me and Mace found a place right over that ridge. We walked here in about a half hour," she admitted.

Tabby's own grin was as big as Kathleen's. "We're neighbours?"

"We're all neighbours," Cade declared as he joined them. "My pack makes their home around a lake just south of here."

"And my pack is about another half hour past Mace's place," James added.

"We're surrounded," Tabby declared as she laughed in delight. "All our friends are close by."

Killian kissed her on the head as he pulled her into his strong arms once more. "It's good to have allies close by. We can help each other when we need it and we can visit whenever we want."

"Sounds perfect," Tabby admitted.

"Plus, when the baby comes you'll have lots of help," Kathleen added.

"What?" Tabby and Killian gasped at the same time.

"When I hugged you I noticed your scent has changed. You're definitely pregnant," Kathleen informed them. "A Wolf's nose can pick up the change almost immediately."

Tabby was in shock, but Killian definitely wasn't. He picked her up, spun her around, and shouted his joy so loud all the packs surrounding them had to have heard.

"Happy?" Killian softly asked once he'd set her back down.

"Ecstatic," Tabby replied. "You saving me was the best thing that ever happened to me."

Epilogue

Killian couldn't remember the last time he was this happy. Meeting his Kitten had definitely changed his life. Never would he have ever imagined he'd love someone as much as her. When he was a soldier he didn't have time for romance, and when he was a Death Angel it wasn't allowed. Falling had brought him Tabby, and he would love her until the day he died.

A loud cry got his attention, and he leaned over his girl to stroke his new son's cheek. Tabby had given birth to a baby boy not twenty minutes ago, and already his son was raising hell. The boy was perfect. He had dark hair that curled around his tiny ears, and eyes that were a striking blue. When he grew up, he'd be fighting the girls off.

All their friends were surrounding them and gushing over his new son. Even Azriel was present, although Killian still hadn't quite forgiven the ass. It was Tabby that insisted he stop punching the man every time he saw him, but he couldn't help it. Even now Azriel sported a black eye, although he was grinning and didn't seem to care in the least. Azriel knew he deserved it, and he simply rolled his eyes every time Killian drew back his arm and nailed him.

"What's his name?" Tansi asked, as her and Piper got close. They were Cade and James' mates. The girls were tight and had adopted Tabby into their circle right away.

"Phoenix," Killian declared. They hadn't discussed names yet. They figured they'd know when they saw the baby, and Phoenix seemed fitting. "Both me and Tabby had to die and go through heartache and loss to get where we are today. And now we have a son, a new life that symbolizes power, strength and renewal."

"I love that," Tabby whispered as tears streamed down her face. "It's perfect."

"And what of the prophecy?" James questioned. "So far it's come true about you two. Do you think Phoenix will bring all the paranormals together and change everything for the better?"

"Only time will tell," Killian huffed. "And I don't care what he does, as long as he lives a life where he's happy and finds love."

"He's already fulfilling the prophecy," Azriel shrugged as he smirked at Killian.

"What the hell does that mean?" Killian demanded.

"Look around," Azriel declared as he held out his arms, spreading them wide to include everyone in the room. "He's already brought paranormals together. We have three Fallen in the room, a werewolf, several Enforcers, a human and an Angel. I'd say that's a good start."

"Well I'll be damned," Cade declared as he chuckled. "If he can accomplish this just by being born, he will be a force to be reckoned with when he's older."

With that conversation ended and the celebrating began. Killian had Tabby, Phoenix and close friends he considered family. He smiled as he watched them all laughing and enjoying each other's company. A lot had changed for him in the hundreds of years he'd been alive. The future was something he now looked forward too, and he couldn't wait to see what it would bring. One thing was for sure though, with this group, it would never be boring.

THE END

The Fallen Angel Series will return...
with Azriel's story.

About the Author

MEGAN FALL is a mother of three who helps her husband run his construction business. She has been writing all her life, but with a push from her daughter started publishing. It's the best thing she ever did. When she's not writing, you can find her at the beach. She loves searching for rocks, sea glass, driftwood and fossils. She believes in ghosts, collects ridiculous amounts of plants, and rides on the back of her hubby's motorcycle.

MEGAN FALL

Look for Megan's other books.

STONE KNIGHTS MC SERIES:
Finding Ali
Saving Cassie
Loving Misty
Rescuing Tiffany
Guarding Alexandria
Protecting Fable
Surviving November
Sheltering Macy
Defending Zoe
Treasuring Maggie (Coming soon)

DEVILS SOLDIERS MC SERIES:
Resisting Diesel
Surviving Hawk (Coming soon)

THE ENFORCER SERIES:
The Enforcer
The Enforcers Revenge

OTHER WORLD SERIES:
Elemental Prince (Coming soon)

THE FALLEN ANGEL SERIES:
Killian

MORE BOOKS TO COME...

Made in United States
North Haven, CT
17 November 2022

26838675R00124